THE PRINCESS AND THE PROPHECY

CURSED: CASSANDRA

OTHER BOOKS

Fated

The Head and the Heart

The Flower and the Flame

The Sorrow and the Sea

Cursed

The Princess and the Prophecy

The Fallow and the Faint

The Weaver and the Web

THE PRINCESS AND THE PROPHECY

CURSED: CASSANDRA

KERRI KEBERLY

Cover design by Keith Robinson

Dragonfire Press

Print ISBN: 978-1-958354-78-0

CHAPTER 1

CASSANDRA SMILED AS she pulled back the string of her bow and aimed the tip of an arrow at a tree. It wasn't customary for women to learn archery, but she was a princess, the daughter of King Priam and Queen Hecuba of Troy, and so she was allowed to bend the rules, especially on her eighteenth name day.

The bow, crafted of sturdy maple and coveted by many a soldier in the Trojan army, had been a gift. Cassandra was accustomed to receiving such fine things from her father's people, but the bow had not been from just anyone.

"Steady now," called out the man standing next to the tree. "Close one eye if you must." The man was striking in appearance, tall and lean-muscled, with burnished curls that shined brightly, even in the dim light of the forest.

It was no wonder they did. He who stood before her was no man, but Apollo, the God of Sun and Light, holding domain over many things, including archery. The bow had been his gift to Cassandra on her sixteenth name day.

Determined to keep both eyes open this time, she zeroed in on a particularly large knot in the bark and let loose her arrow. It pierced through the rough outer layer and sunk deep into the heart of the tree. She lowered her bow, sending Apollo a triumphant grin.

"A fluke," he teased, shaking his head in amusement at her capricious nature as he pulled the arrow out as easily as though he were plucking fruit.

Cassandra's heart danced in her chest, her cheeks warming at the display of raw power. Oh, what she wouldn't give to possess some of it. Alas, she had not been born a goddess, and suspected the reason the god of music and dancing and poetry favored her was for her beauty, certainly, but more importantly, her cleverness.

"Perhaps I shall go again," shouted Cassandra, "to prove you wrong." She withdrew another arrow from the quiver strapped to her back. She felt brave enough to cajole the god in this way. He'd been visiting her for two years, after all.

Though many months had passed, she remembered their first encounter like it was the day before. It had been a lovely morning, much like this one, sunny and mild, with a slight breeze to lift the ends of her dark mahogany hair. She and her twin brother, Helenus, had been practicing shooting arrows at this very spot. After a few hours, her brother had gone in search of bread and cheese to fill his growling belly, but Cassandra had stayed behind, shooting her arrows until blisters formed on her fingers. She had always been headstrong, and she was determined to surpass her brother's naturally good marksmanship.

Now, she nocked an arrow on the very same bow Apollo had given her that day, ready to take aim, when a vision of Helenus approaching from behind flashed in her mind's eye. On her seventeenth name day, Apollo had given her the gift of foresight. Thanks to her, Helenus had received it as well.

"I see your aim has gotten better," her brother shouted from afar.

She lowered her bow at the sound of his voice, whirling around and pretending to be startled.

Helenus chuckled. "There is no need for show, sister. Not with our minds. How do you think I knew you would be here? Besides, I was noisier than a wild boar barging through the brush."

"It was not a difficult thing to know," she replied, a bit indignant. She loved Helenus dearly, but things had always come easy to him. He'd been born a boy, affording him more liberties than her from the moment they left the womb. It irked her at times like this, when he patronized her. "I always come here on our name day."

What she did not say aloud was she always came on this day, to this spot, to receive whatever gift Apollo would bestow upon her. He would appear at other times, of course, but meeting here on her name day had become a tradition so he could give her a gift. It had been the bow first, followed by foresight the next year. She was anxious to know what her eighteenth name day gift would be.

Some days she wondered if she should have kept the foresight to herself instead of sharing it. She'd agreed to accept it on the condition that her twin would receive the same. She didn't know why she'd done it, but it wasn't for Helenus's sake, that much she knew. She supposed she'd done it to see how far Apollo would go, and exactly how much of his divine power she could talk him into giving her.

But, at times like this, when Helenus made it difficult to ever be alone, she regretted it.

Cassandra glanced back at the tree where Apollo had been standing. The arrow stuck out of its thick trunk, but, as always when anyone else approached unexpectedly, the god had vanished. Apollo only showed himself to her, which was an honor she cherished, but it made her behavior seem rather strange to the others, even Helenus at times. For all the foresight he possessed, he had no idea it was because *she* was favored by Apollo.

As close as they were, she didn't think Helenus could suspend such disbelief. She'd tried broaching the subject once, and although he agreed their gift was divine, he refused to acknowledge that it had been bestowed upon them because his sister had caught the eye of the God of Prophecy himself. He or her parents or her maid would see her talking to herself often, but they could not fathom she could be conversing with the divine.

4

She had tried to explain this many times, that she was favored by one of the very gods who built their city's impenetrable walls, but they all chose to believe she simply had the wildest of imaginations. This seemed strange to Cassandra, especially given that her own mother was said to sometimes have prophetic dreams.

"It's a good thing archers rely on their eyes and not their ears, dear brother," replied Cassandra, dismissing the thought and hoping her remark was enough of a segue. "What brings you out here to interrupt my practice?"

The smile dropped from his face. She hated when her brother went serious like this. It meant only one thing.

"I've come to ask if you've seen him," he replied.

Cassandra swallowed hard, knowing the man her brother spoke of. The shepherd. The one on his way to the festival their father hosted each year. The one who looked so much like their older brother Hector that they, too, could be twins.

"Yes," she said, barely audible. Suddenly, her eyes glazed as a vision overtook her mind. The way the shepherd laughed with his traveling companions, free and easy and heartily. Though it didn't happen as often now that he had grown older, this was the way their father laughed.

Without warning, the vision of the young man switched to their mother, sweaty from labor. She cried as she held a newborn baby, but they were not tears of joy. Anguish crumpled her features as she stroked a shock of dark hair before a nursemaid whisked the baby away.

Cassandra blinked away both the tears and the vision. One look at Helenus's wide eyes and furrowed brow and she knew he'd seen it, too. She and Helenus had heard the stories whispered among the palace maids of a stillborn baby who had come only a few years before her and Helenus's birth, and how Hecuba did not leave her rooms for months.

"He lives," she whispered. "Our brother lives."

CHAPTER 2

THE SUN HAD gone down and the palace had settled into sleep long ago, but Cassandra lay awake, her troubled mind racing. Why had her mother and father given away their child? Did he know he was a prince of Troy? Is that why he makes his way to the festival? Why had Apollo not visited? Was he angry with her?

She stared into the darkness of her room, scouring memories of the day and going over all she'd said and done in the hope of discovering some offence she had committed. Apollo could be unpredictable in his moods, but he had never simply abandoned her like this before. If anything, it seemed she had grown more endeared to him with each time he came to her, which had been more and more often over the past year. The way he smiled fondly and playfully bantered with her certainly seemed to suggest he would not be put off so easily.

She shivered under the layers of her night gown. The other thing that kept her from sleep was the visions that her and Helenus had shared. Unlike Cassandra, Helenus didn't have them often, and they were usually something harmless and trivial, like what would be served for the evening meal.

Unease had been swirling in her belly ever since her brother had come to her in the wood earlier that day. They had both found the visions to be ominous, but where she wanted to confront their parents, Helenus was unwilling to broach the subject with them, instead begging her to keep what they had seen to themselves.

"We should not meddle in the affairs of the gods, sister," he'd said as they had made their way back to the palace. She'd wanted to stay, but Helenus had been so shaken there would have been no way she could have remained in the woods to wait for Apollo without raising suspicion.

"There must be a reason for it," he'd continued. "If mother and father notice the resemblance, so be it, but we should stay out of it. You see the looks of reproach they give you when you behave so strangely."

"I told you," Cassandra had snapped in reply, "Apollo speaks to me."

"I believe you," he'd said, raising his eyebrows at her. "But no one else does. They see you as seeking attention."

Cassandra folded her arms to cover up the sting of hurt she felt at the truth. "Is that how *you* see it?"

"Not anymore," he had said, shaking his head vigorously. "I now know the gift we've inherited from our mother is both a blessing and a curse. It was amusing before, when all I saw made sense and was harmless."

Cassandra didn't agree with keeping quiet about what they'd seen. The shepherd was their long-lost sibling, cast aside for reasons unknown, but seeing how unsettled it made Helenus, she had promised not to say a word.

The festival was to begin in two days. Perhaps when her parents saw this man who bore the features of so many of Priam's sons at the games, they would make the connection on their own, rejoice and welcome him back into the fold with open arms, and neither Cassandra nor Helenus need point it out.

She yawned, her mind finally slowing enough for her lids to grow heavy.

Like tinder catching fire, a light suddenly flared to life, breaking through the darkness of sleep. Had morning come so soon? Cassandra groaned at the thought, burrowing deeper into her bed. She hadn't gotten nearly enough rest to face the day of overthinking that awaited her.

A shudder rippled through her, bringing her senses into sharper focus. The chill of night still hung in the air, and the crickets still chirped outside her window. Her skin prickled, and when the hazy reddish glow behind her still closed eyelids pulsed, as though it were keeping time with a beating heart, she knew morning had not come. It was something—someone—else.

"Cassandra," came a voice. It was rich in timber and smooth in pitch, and one she knew well by now.

Her eyes flew open, and there, standing at the foot of her bed, bathed in light, was Apollo. She sat up, eager to ask what had taken him so long, why he had waited until now to appear, but he glowed so radiantly she remained silent, instead lifting her hand to shield her eyes.

The tunic he wore was different, shorter, and she couldn't keep her gaze from sweeping over his broad chest down to his strong bared thighs and back to his languid smile. She had seen him smile many times before, but there was something in the way the edges of it curled higher on one side that made her breath quicken. And his eyes, they seemed darker, peering at her through half closed lids so intensely it made her cheeks warm.

She had always thought him pleasing, but as a brother, even a father figure. The way he looked at her now was not how a brother looked at a sister, or a father at a daughter, and she was ashamed how her body responded to his smoldering gaze.

"I've come to give you your gift," he said, moving toward her.

Her palms went slick with sweat when she glanced down at his hands only to find there was nothing in them. No arrows for her bow. No musical instrument to learn. Not even a pristine white calf from his herd of divine cattle.

Perhaps he intended to recite a poem he had written especially for her?

Her heart pounded in her ears, and her breath hitched when he sat on the edge of her bed. They had been this close before, but never in such an intimate setting. He had always visited her in the daylight, never once in the darkness of her room.

She swallowed hard. She knew what happened between men and women in the dark.

"What is it?" she asked, trying to keep the quaver from her voice.

He laughed, low and amused. "Me."

"You?" she replied. "I don't understand."

"I think you understand perfectly well what I mean, Cassandra." The tone of his voice was not harsh, but the reproach in it was clear.

He had never spoken to her this way, with the air between them charged with something so unfamiliar, and it frightened her.

He reached out and caressed her cheek. When his fingers trailed down her neck and over her collarbone, pushing aside her sleeping gown to bare her shoulder, her heart sank. Fear was replaced by anger; all this time she had thought it was her intelligence, that he favored her for her mind and not her body. He had been grooming her for this moment.

This change between them was unwelcome. He sought only to satisfy his lust, and it made her clench her jaw. If she was to give something up, then why shouldn't he?

Her mind raced as she stared at him, thinking of what she should ask for in return. She was hurt and angry and desperately wanted him to leave so she could pretend this advance had never happened, so they could go back to the way they were, but that wasn't likely. He was a god, one who believed he was owed for gracing her with his presence and bestowing upon her gifts she hadn't asked for.

Cassandra steeled herself. If he could take what he wanted, then why couldn't she?

"I'm not worthy," she said, trying one last time to reason with him before telling him the price he must pay to have her.

"If you were not worthy, I would have never given you the gift of foresight."

Straightening her spine, she commanded the swirling in her belly to cease. "If I am to be claimed by you, then I must be a goddess."

"No. That's impossible," he replied, shaking his head.

"Why?"

"It is Zeus and Zeus alone who can gift immortality," he said.

Cassandra lifted her chin. "Then go to him and make the request."

"It's not as simple as that," he said, raking a hand through his golden curls. "He does not favor me enough."

She folded her arms. "Then I remain untouched."

Apollo growled in frustration, one fist coming down hard on the mat beside her. "You are being petulant. I gave you what you wanted, and now..." He leaned in, until his lips were a hair's breadth away from hers. "It's time for you to return the favor."

"Not unless I go from princess to goddess."

Apollo said nothing, his expression unreadable. When the muscle over his jaw clenched, Cassandra dropped her defensive stance, hoping she hadn't gone too far.

"Hmmm," said Apollo, lifting her chin with a forefinger so he could inspect the line of her jaw. "Such a tempting bargain." He gently brushed his thumb over her bottom lip, pulling it down to expose her tongue and teeth. "Do you tell the truth, Cassandra?" His fingers slid along her cheek, threading through her hair until they came to rest at the base of her skull. "Or are you a silver-tongued liar?"

She opened her mouth to speak, to take back the demand she'd made, but she didn't get the chance.

"I think it's the latter," he whispered softly. "And as the purveyor of truth, I don't much care for liars." He stared directly into her eyes, his gaze dark as a storm cloud. "I cannot take back the gift I have given you, but I can make it suit your true nature."

With that, he pulled her mouth toward his, setting upon her a fury of lips and teeth and tongue. She pushed against him, trying to break free, but it was no use. Her head and hair were in the tight grip of a powerful god. She dared not struggle, lest he steal the breath from her lungs and end her life.

He pressed against her, groping and kissing her so hard and so long, saliva dribbled out the sides of her mouth. Her stomach turned and only when she retched did he stop.

He leaned back, swiping the spittle from his own mouth with the back of his hand.

"There," he said, his nostrils flaring with indignance. "That should do it. Enjoy your final gift from me, Cassandra."

Nearly suffocated, she gulped down precious air as the light surrounding Apollo dimmed. The god who'd once favored her faded away to nothing, until she was alone in the dark once more.

CHAPTER 3

THE SUN BLAZED down on the royal platform without mercy. Apollo was punishing her; Cassandra was sure of it. If it had not been for the swath of thick canvas draped overhead, she would have melted away. Part of her wished she *would* dissolve, growing smaller and smaller until she was nothing. It would be a reprieve from agonizing over what Apollo's last words to her had truly meant.

Enjoy your final gift from me, Cassandra.

It had been a thoughtful enough sentiment, but Cassandra did not miss the malice in his words. She knew the gods held their grudges for ages. The nursemaids had told her the stories. And now she was on the precipice of being a cautionary tale herself, recounted to future generations. For Apollo had given her nothing she could see or touch, but the dark and sinister look that had flashed in his deep blue eyes had proven he had not given her a gift at all, but a curse.

What it was, she had yet to discover.

She'd lost sleep thinking about what sort of terrible punishment might befall her and for how long. Although Apollo had left her maidenhood intact those few nights ago, the retribution for refusing him was not over. He would find a way to torture her through cruel and unusual ways for the rest of her life.

Several young men ran past the platform where she and Helenus, their brothers Hector and Deiphobus, and the king and queen sat on cushioned stools. Cassandra coughed from the dust dredged up by swift feet, wishing she were anywhere else but watching a group of boys and men engage in competitions against each other. She could slip away during the feasting and drinking that would take place later that evening, but for now, Cassandra would have to endure both the filth and the heat of the afternoon. Worse, she'd have to find a way to survive the incessant boasting of contestants and subsequent cheering from the crowd for the winners.

Like the cloth above her head, the veil covering her face did little to protect her from her discomforts. She sighed, careful to keep the stoic façade of royalty, just as Hecuba had taught her. Truth be told, she'd much rather be in her room, out from under the scrutiny of Apollo, even if it meant waiting for him to come to her and explain exactly what kind of terrible punishment she must suffer.

But she already knew he would not be divulging such details any time soon, if ever. Apollo was the god of prophecy, and prophecies must be puzzled out.

When it was time for the showing of bulls to begin, Cassandra straightened in her seat, leaning forward to get a better look at the man entering the ring. It was the shepherd.

She watched as he led a black steer with long horns up to the platform for inspection. Afterward, the massive beast would be put inside a holding pen to wait. Once the second bull was introduced, the first would be unleashed, set upon each other to see which of them was the strongest, with the winner advancing through the ranks until there was only one bull left. Once an ultimate victor had been called, it would be sacrificed.

It seemed a rather terrible and sad thing for such a hard-won victory to be rewarded with death, but the gods demanded it. The best and most cherished must always be offered to them.

Cassandra swallowed hard before looking over at Helenus. He had gone pale, and she immediately switched her gaze to her father. His brow was furrowed, eyes narrowed and fixed on the shepherd, as if trying to recall where he'd seen the man before.

She looked at Hecuba next, who stared wide-eyed and unblinking at the young man standing before them. She saw the resemblance.

A low murmur rippled through the crowd. They all saw it.

The shepherd was almost as tall as Hector. Their older brother's features were dark and rugged, the shepherd's more handsome and refined but just as dark, nonetheless. She glanced at Deiphobus, another of her brothers. Skepticism etched his face into hard lines and sharp angles, but she knew he could see the other obvious family trait plain as day. The dark chestnut hair that both Helenus and Cassandra possessed. They had inherited it from Hecuba.

Cassandra bit the inside of her cheek until she tasted blood. She switched to the other side, her teeth clamping down on unmarred flesh as the shepherd bowed his head before introducing himself.

"I am Paris, son of Agelaus," he began. "And I am honored to show you the best among my father's stock. What Ares has left of it, anyway." He chuckled to himself, at the jest only he was privy to, before gesturing toward the bull pawing impatiently at the dusty ground. "This is Nikitis."

Winner. Not only did the shepherd look like a son of Priam, but he spoke with the cocksure confidence of one.

"A son of Agelaus, did you say? The old shepherd?" replied Priam, shifting in his chair.

"Well, a son in name if not by blood," answered Paris. "I know he bore hair the color of gold before it turned silver. I am as dark featured as..." His eyes cut to Hector, Deiphobus, then Helenus and, finally, Cassandra.

Did this man know the truth, that he was a son of Priam and Hecuba?

Cassandra suddenly felt lightheaded, a thrumming, like the beating of a drum, filling her ears. She looked around, but no one seemed to hear it. She decided it must be the heat, until she saw the way her mother clutched at her dress, balling the fabric tightly in her fists.

Cassandra's head jerked back, her eyes rolling in their sockets. "He lives," she blurted, unable to stop herself. It was as though she were another person entirely. "The one you abandoned. Paris is a son of Troy!"

"Nonsense, girl," said Priam. "Stop your babbling."

One of Hecuba's hands shot out, gripping Priam's forearm for balance.

"Could it be?" she whispered.

Priam reached over and laid his hand on hers. "No, my darling, it's impossible. I gave Agelaus strict orders."

Cassandra's head whirled toward Helenus.

His lips were pressed into a thin line before he opened them to mouth the words, *"You promised!"*

"It wasn't me!" she whispered, frantically trying to explain.

Helenus shot her a look of anger before huffing loudly. He had seen the same vision. He knew as well as she did Paris was their long-lost brother, and although she had been unable to control herself from speaking, the truth was out, and there was no way anyone could pretend Paris was a lowly shepherd from the hills.

"She speaks the truth," he said, his tone more commanding than she'd ever heard it before. "Your son lives."

Cassandra thought for a moment that Helenus was going to explain how he was so sure, but there was no need. Priam's creased brow smoothed, as though Helenus's words simply wiped away all disbelief. Hecuba had let go of her husband's arm to cover her mouth.

Priam looked at his wife for permission. She nodded and he cleared his throat.

"Good people of Troy..." he began. "Twenty-two years ago, my wife had a dream. She saw a burning torch."

Hecuba stifled a sob.

Cassandra's throat burned as though she had swallowed a mouthful of stinging nettles only to spew forth a torrent of venom. The lump forming in her throat grew, aching with pent up screams.

Why had her father believed Helenus and not her?

"When the seer Aesacus confirmed the child born would need to be—"

"We gave up the child to spare the kingdom," cut in Hecuba, having regained her composure. She slipped back into the role of reigning queen instead of grieving mother.

"What Queen Hecuba says is true, we had no choice," continued Priam, raising his voice over the excited murmuring of the crowd. "But it seems it is the gods' will that our son should be returned to us."

Hector, seated next to their father, eyed Paris with as much suspicion as Deiphobus. "With all due respect, father, what proof do we have this man is who you think he is?"

"You're right, Hector," said Priam, nodding slowly. "There must be proof." He turned toward Paris. "Please join us at the royal table this evening. There is much to discuss."

"Of course," said Paris, smiling broadly. "I shall be honored."

Without warning, an image of a city on fire took over Cassandra's senses. It was so real, as though she were there, in the middle of the destruction. The screams of men rose goose flesh on her arms, and the smell of burning hair made her wretch. She clutched the edges of her stool for support, but her grip was powerless to stop the cry of horror that burst from her lips when she saw something truly terrifying.

She shook her head. "No... No!"

It was Troy. She knew from the banners being ravaged by fire it was her beloved city besieged. They bore the symbol of her brother Hector, a white horse, to signify the greatest warrior their city had.

Hecuba turned in her seat to face her.

"Cassandra? What is wrong with you?"

She could not get the words out. She saw things, having been granted the power to see the future, and she'd just seen their beloved city on fire. She groaned, shaking her head more violently. How was it possible? Troy's walls were impenetrable. Her father had said so. They had been built by Poseidon and...

Apollo.

She screamed.

Apollo.

The divinity who had given her the gift of foresight.

Hecuba nodded at two handmaids sitting below the platform. "Cassandra has been in the sun too long. Escort her back to her room."

She dropped her head into her hands, waiting to be lifted by her arms and led away.

CHAPTER 4

CASSANDRA STARED BLEARY-EYED at the stone wall before her, waiting for her mind to replay the horrible chain of events that had led to her confinement. It had been a relief when she'd been escorted back to her room, and she had gladly stayed there for the duration of the festival, but she was anxious to leave it now that a few days had passed.

She couldn't bear to be alone with her thoughts anymore. They were relentless, playing over and over in her mind and robbing her of sleep. She was exhausted, and the only sense she had managed to make of the terrible vision was that Troy would burn. But she did not know how or why or when, and that meant more visions would come.

Lost in thought, she didn't bother to turn her head when there came a knock.

"Come in."

Two handmaids entered with clay jars of steaming water in each hand. She said nothing as they looked at her with wary eyes as they poured her a bath. They helped her into the tub before setting to work on washing away the gritty dirt and dried sweat coating her skin. The hot water felt good, and she silently thanked her mother for ordering that she be bathed.

Once she was dressed in clean clothes, and her hair was coiled and pinned, the women finally left. Still a bit dazed and confused, Cassandra sat on the edge of her bed. Was this how the seer Aesacus felt after he'd had a vision, untethered and delusional? It couldn't be—the prophecies he foretold were taken seriously.

Tears suddenly formed in her eyes, panic seizing her. Perhaps she was simply going mad.

She shook away the thought. No. No, she was not going mad. She was fine. Everything was going to be fine.

Determined to be strong, she dried her eyes, dabbing carefully with her finger so she wouldn't smear the kohl lining them. When she heard shouts coming from outside, she stood and made her way over to the only window in her room. It overlooked the back courtyard. The tents where the contestants had stayed were gone, leaving bare patches of dirt where their feet had worn away the grass.

They had all left. All but one.

Her brother Paris.

She watched silently as Paris and one of her other brothers, Troilus, circled each other, sizing one another up as the king and queen looked on from cushioned chairs. Helenus stood behind them, along with Hector and Deiphobus. When her twin spotted her, he waved, beckoning for her to come join them.

Cassandra sighed before turning to leave her room. They must have decided a wrestling match was how they would determine whether Paris was a prince of Troy. It would prove nothing but skill and endurance, not reveal anything whatsoever about whose blood ran through Paris's veins.

But she supposed her parents were desperate for confirmation, needing to assuage their guilt somehow. She scoffed as she made her way down a flight of stairs, more than one servant scared off by her muttering as she made her way through the palace. They had all the proof they needed. Their own daughter had *seen* the truth. Paris was indeed their long-lost son.

Cassandra walked across the courtyard, taking a place next to Helenus just as Paris pinned Troilus to the ground. Cassandra winced, feeling sorry for Troilus. He was red-faced and panting, his body contorted into a very uncomfortable looking position. Paris hadn't even broken a sweat.

They all clapped lightly, the king a bit more loudly than the others. "Well done, Paris!"

"Yes, well done, *shepherd*," mocked Deiphobus. "I'm sure your bulls have given you ample practice at wrestling."

"Deiphobus," said Hector, shifting from leaning on his spear with one ankle crossed over the other to standing at the ready should Deiphobus decide to get out of hand. "Let's not resort to insults."

Hecuba turned to send Deiphobus a reproachful look as Paris released Troilus and stood.

"Good match," said Paris, offering his hand. Troilus took it, and Paris pulled him to his feet and clapped him on the back.

Deiphobus snickered, his gaze still trained on Paris as he spoke. "What shall we resort to, now? Herding?"

Hector shot Deiphobus a look of warning.

"I'll fight any of you, even Hector." Paris shrugged. "I'll fight you, Deiphobus, if that is what you wish. I'm not afraid."

Cassandra stepped closer to Helenus. Hector could keep his wits about him under the pressure of a challenge, but Deiphobus's hot temper made him rash and unpredictable. There was no telling what Deiphobus would do when threatened.

Deiphobus went to step forward, but Hector stopped him. "You try my patience. You will cause no more grief on this matter, whatever the outcome."

Cassandra flinched when Hector wrenched Deiphobus's spear from his hand before stepping toward Paris.

"I mean you no offense, Paris, but it is true that the sons of Troy are fighters," said Hector. "I say to the gods now, if Paris is a son of Priam, then show us the proof." He tossed Deiphobus's spear to Paris, who caught it with ease. "Defeat me, and we will *all*," Hector called over his shoulder, "accept you as a son and brother of Troy."

Cassandra held her breath as the men advanced toward one another. She tried to keep her posture relaxed, but she could not stop her shoulders from creeping up and her back from hunching with her desire to look away. Although this would not be a fight to the death, she loved Hector dearly and didn't want to see him wounded.

Hector had boldly asked the gods to show them the truth. Cassandra knew they would, and she knew firsthand how callously they could answer.

Cassandra watched as each blow was blocked until her vision blurred. She blinked to clear it, then gasped when there stood Apollo, just beyond where Hector and Paris parried each other's strikes.

He stared at her, expressionless.

She stepped closer to Helenus, gripping the back of his tunic. "Do you see him?"

"See who, sister?" he said, reaching behind to gently pry open her fingers.

"Apollo," she whispered. "Don't you see him standing there?"

"There is no one there, Cassandra," said Helenus, pulling away from her. "Stop this, sister."

Helenus might have said more, but Cassandra did not hear it. All she heard was the strange pulsing hum she'd heard at the festival. And all she saw was Apollo, and the way he smiled at her before, quick as lightning, flicking his hand.

She gasped when, infused with the power of the gods, Paris knocked the spear out of Hector's iron grip. Taking advantage of his shock, Paris swept Hector's feet out from under him, and then lunged forward so the tip of the spear rested mere inches from Hector's heart.

After a tense moment, Hector smiled up at Paris and nodded.

Paris removed the tip of the spear and, reaching down, helped Troy's greatest warrior to his feet.

Apollo had vanished, his meddling done, leaving Cassandra to sway unsteadily, knowing full well what would come next but hoping Paris would have the smallest sliver of decorum to restrain himself.

"Are you satisfied now..." said Paris, turning toward Deiphobus and grinning. "Brother."

"You are not my brother!" shouted Deiphobus, trying to shake off Helenus, who'd sprung forward just in time to catch Deiphobus before he could charge. "Hector is my brother. Troilus, Helenus, they are my brothers. You, Paris, are *not my brother.*"

"Silence!" bellowed Priam, raising his staff high in the air.

The clanging of bells and faint lowing floated on the breeze. The sound of clacking hooves and turning wheels broke through the trees, and a few moments later a pair of oxen pulling a wooden cart appeared.

After the driver pulled the animals to a halt, he hopped down to help an old man out of the back of the cart.

"Agelaus?" called out Paris, dropping the spear and breaking out into a run. "What are you doing here?"

"Your companions returned with news that a claim of legitimacy had been made," replied Agelaus. "Since it seems the cat is out of the bag, my dear boy, I have come to lay to rest any doubt that you are a son of Priam."

By now, they had all made their way over to Agelaus, wondering how the old shepherd planned to prove anything.

Agelaus looked at Priam and Hecuba. "Nine days. That is how long he survived. I did as you asked and left him, but it was not the gods' will that he should perish. When I went back, he was pink-cheeked and healthy. I dared not go against the gods, and so I raised him as my own."

Agelaus handed Paris his walking staff before untying a purse attached to the waist of his tunic. A muffled rattling, like beans trapped inside a jar, made Cassandra's heart thud in her chest. When the old man pulled out a baby's toy, clay molded into the shape of a horse, she clamped her mouth shut. It was a toy they all had played with as children, even Hector. It was the Trojan horse, and there were dozens around the palace, still played with by the younger children of Priam and Hecuba.

Agelaus handed Hecuba the rattle. "Paris does indeed belong to Troy."

Hecuba's mouth had fallen agape. Irritation gnawed at Cassandra. How many times had her mother told Cassandra to keep herself in check, to never show such open displays of emotion? And here the Queen of Troy stood, not even trying to hide one so uncouth as shock.

Why was Hecuba surprised? Cassandra had already told them the truth.

Cassandra clenched her jaw when Hecuba took Paris's face in her hands, and she ground her teeth when an unrestrained smile reached her mother's tear-filled eyes.

"Welcome home, my son."

The words barely left her mother's mouth when a vision seized Cassandra's mind. It was of Paris, leading a young woman wearing a thin circlet of gold by the hand through the gates of Troy. Once through, he bent to kiss the woman, and the city behind them burst into flames.

Cassandra stifled her own cry. It was not of joy, but of anguish, and she pinched her thigh with all the strength her fingers could muster in a desperate attempt to stop herself from screaming.

CHAPTER 5

CASSANDRA WALKED THROUGH the torchlit corridor beside Helenus, neither saying a word to the other. He had tried to strike up a conversation, and she had tried to humor him, but all she had managed were a few soft grunts and then a slight shrug when he'd asked her if she was well. Unsure how to pull her from melancholy, he'd stopped talking. The only sounds either of them heard now were the scuffing of feet on stone and the hiss of torches lighting their way.

So be it, she was preoccupied with preparing for another night of everyone in attendance fawning over Paris to truly care.

It wasn't that she didn't *like* Paris. He was her brother, after all, with an agreeable temperament like most of her other siblings. He didn't speak harshly to her or treat her poorly in the weeks since his return.

She simply didn't trust him.

And it seemed he felt the same. It could have been her silence whenever he entered the room, or her refusal to lavish an endless stream of compliments on him like the others, but with every sideways glance he sent her, it was apparent he was just as wary of her as she was of him.

Did he know she saw things the others did not, like when he'd handed Ares a crown made of gold? Or when he placed a shining golden apple in Aphrodite's hand? Cassandra didn't know what these things meant, only that no one would believe her if she said them aloud.

And so, she kept her distance and remained silent. Despite her growing list of reservations, and what it meant now that Paris was back home, days at the palace had been lively and dinners had been full of merriment. She could not remember a time when she'd seen her parents so carefree with their laughter.

Despite her parents' happiness bringing immense joy to her own heart, it annoyed Cassandra that Paris was all anyone could talk about.

"He is so comely and magnanimous, so well-spoken and poised!"

Even proud Deiphobus was enamored with Paris. He went on and on about the fight with Hector, recounting every detail of the now infamous contest in the courtyard. Cassandra couldn't help but roll her eyes every time he launched into another retelling of the story.

She knew full well Paris's skill with a spear had been on lend from Apollo. Blessedly, Hector only laughed, secure enough in his role as Troy's heir and greatest warrior to ignore Deiphobus's ribbing.

She and Helenus entered the dining room and took their seats at the table. At Hecuba's insistence, the custom of men and women dining separately had been abandoned, for the evening meal, at least. Priam had offered no protest.

Cassandra glanced over the bronze bowls of soup, loaves of unleavened bread, and silver platters of fish, fruit, cheese, and olives, toward the head of the table. Her mother and father sat side-by-side, with Hector seated to the king's right. Deiphobus sat next to Paris, who sat at Hecuba's left side, filling the role as second son.

Cassandra turned to Helenus. "Have you had anymore visions, brother?"

Helenus tilted his head in consternation. "Come to think of it, no, I haven't seen anything since Paris arrived. Have you?"

She kept her voice casual and light, hoping what she was about to say sounded convincing. "Nothing like what we saw together."

Not a lie, exactly, but certainly not the whole truth.

Helenus arched an eyebrow at her. "Are you sure? You have been acting strangely. You're more quiet than usual. What vexes you?"

Cassandra's stomach looped. In all the world, there was no one who knew her as well as Helenus. She could not lie to him even if she wanted to.

"I don't trust him."

"Who?" said Helenus around a mouthful of bread. "Paris?"

"Shhh!" Cassandra gave him a slight nod, looking around to see if anyone was listening to their conversation. She was relieved to see that no one was paying her or Helenus any mind. All eyes were on Paris, and in this instance, Cassandra was glad for his ability to hold the attention of an entire room.

"Cassandra, he is our brother," said Helenus. "There is no reason for mistrust."

"But..." How could Cassandra explain her suspicions when, lately, every word that came out of her mouth was taken as nonsense. "He was not raised as a prince of Troy. How do we know he does not intend to challenge Hector for the throne?"

Helenus shook his head. "Cassandra," he laughed. "Stop this. Paris has nothing but good intentions."

It was no use. Not even Helenus would see to reason. Cassandra nearly choked on an olive when she heard Paris casually ask her father about Troy's relationship with Sparta.

She forced her gaze to remain on her dinner plate, pretending she couldn't hear the conversation starting down at the other end of the table. But the room had gone silent, everyone, including her, listening intently.

King Priam shrugged. "We offered hospitality to King Menelaus not long ago, so it is currently an amenable one, I suppose. Why do you ask?"

"What reason did he give for invoking *Xenia*?" asked Paris.

"He did not say directly," replied Priam, "but insinuated it was the duty of neighboring kings to ensure a peaceful co-existence."

"I could not wait until those brutish *Achaeans* left," said Hecuba, not bothering to hide her disgust.

Priam nodded. "It was most uncomfortable, I agree, but the rules of *Xenia* were not to be broken."

"Are you suggesting Menelaus only came to see how gullible Troy is?" Deiphobus asked Paris.

"That is exactly what I am suggesting."

"He's right," said Hector. "I have expressed this many times. The only reason why Menelaus's brother Agamemnon leaves Troy untouched is because they have not yet unified the Greek states. But Agamemnon is as ruthless as he is persistent, and Menelaus is loyal to his brother. They work to build a monarchy even as we speak. Make no mistake, once they amass a powerful enough army, they will come for Troy."

"Let them," said Hecuba, lifting her chin. "Troy's walls cannot be breeched."

"That may be true, but the Greeks are cunning," said Paris. "Menelaus did not take Sparta by force."

"They took it by marriage," said Priam, nodding slowly with understanding.

"Why Helen chose that ugly brute Menelaus I will never know," scoffed Hecuba. "It must have been the work of the gods."

Suddenly, the image of the woman Cassandra had seen Paris kiss flashed behind her eyes. It was quick, and when it was over her gaze cut to him just in time for her to see his throat bob nervously.

"Yes, and if we are not careful," said Hector, glancing at Cassandra. "We may find ourselves married to our enemy."

"If we want to know their next move, we must play their game," said Paris.

"Are you saying we ally with them?" asked Hecuba.

Cassandra swallowed hard. Aligning with the *Achaeans* would be lowering themselves, which was unthinkable to the Trojans. They had been a people unto their own for hundreds of years, protected by the gods who built their city's formidable walls. Troy was superior in every way, and to ally with such crude and barbaric people would be a colossal insult, not only to the Trojan way of life but to the gods who protected it.

Why would Paris even suggest it?

"Not exactly, but we must outwit them. Let me go to Sparta, to see what I can learn of Menelaus and Agamemnon's true feelings toward Troy."

"You've only just returned to us, Paris," said Hecuba.

"And already I offer to sacrifice my safety so that Troy remains impervious to the infiltration of the Greeks," replied Paris. "I'll take Hector with me. There is no way Menelaus would break *Xenia* with two sons of Troy in his palace."

Helenus leaned over and whispered. "See? He campaigns for the wellbeing of Troy, not the throne."

Cassandra swallowed the olive she'd been chewing just as the strange thrumming noise filled her head. She did not answer Helenus, only narrowed her eyes at Paris, seeing right through him. The crowned woman in her vision had been Spartan. Paris did not go to Sparta for diplomacy.

He went for its queen.

CHAPTER 6

THE VISION OF Paris handing a golden apple to Aphrodite ran through Cassandra's head as she stormed through the palace. The images had been tormenting her for three days, making more sense each time she had seen more of what had transpired.

Hera, Athena, and Aphrodite gather at a wedding, whose Cassandra could not say, but the goddess of strife, Eris, tosses a golden apple into the air above them.

To the fairest...

Cassandra's footsteps pounded in time with her heart as she made her way to the place where Paris was sure to be, in Priam's private sitting room, finalizing the list of provisions needed for his envoy to Sparta.

Each goddess clambers for it, but Zeus snatches it away. He knows the terrible quarrel it will cause, but not wanting to be responsible for settling the matter, he decrees Paris to be the judge. Feeling as though it is an honor, Paris agrees.

Then, each goddess promises Paris something—Hera offers power, Athena victory,

Aphrodite a lifetime of love and lust with the most beautiful woman known to man—in exchange for the apple that supposedly proves who among them is most comely.

Unable to resist her offer, Paris places the apple in Aphrodite's palm.

As much as she wished it weren't so, she must talk to him. How dare her own flesh and blood resort to such trickery, going to Sparta under the guise of diplomacy when his true intention was to collect his prize. It was vital she convince him to abandon his plans to go to Sparta, beseeching him to stay away from its queen, for if he did not, Troy would burn.

Cassandra stomped down the corridor with the jug of wine she'd wrenched out of a stunned servant's hands. She had to have a reason for interrupting, or the guards would never let her into the room during such important business, princess or not.

This enraged her even more.

Cassandra slowed her gait, inhaling a calming breath before approaching the anti-chamber that led to her father's private rooms.

She smiled sweetly as she walked up to the guardsmen.

"I wish to speak with my father," said Cassandra when the king's guard automatically barred her from entry. "I brought refreshment..." She lifted the handled wine jug. "Their throats must be terribly dry from all the preparations they discuss." Still, the guards did not move, only eyed her with skepticism. She demurred, looking at her feet before peering back up with them with teary forlorn eyes. "In truth, I wish to say goodbye to my brothers. Paris, especially, for I have only just gotten to know him."

They nodded their heads at the mere mention of the beloved scoundrel, and one of them stepped aside, turning to open the door so she could enter. Cassandra walked into the room slowly.

Where should she start? *How* should she start?

Priam sat, as did Hector, but Paris stalked around a table littered with strips of papyrus, going over how long he thought he'd need to stay—at least a month—to glean as much information as possible, the more the better.

When the men finally noticed her, their discussion quieted.

"Forgive me for interrupting," she said, gripping the *amphora's* handles tightly so she would not blurt out her accusations, but remain calm enough to explain her intrusion from start to finish. "But I bring wine."

Her father and Hector stared back at her patiently, not surprised by the disturbance in the slightest. They were used to Cassandra's adventurous spirit. Paris, however, was taken aback, confusion etching his face for an instant before he sighed and pinched the bridge of his nose in exasperation.

"Thank you, Cassandra," said Priam, nodding toward an empty space on the table. "You may leave it there."

Despite her father's instruction, Cassandra remained rooted to the spot where she stood, her legs refusing to comply. When an image of Paris kissing the Spartan woman flashed, she bit back a gasp, her body going rigid with the effort.

"Cassandra?" said Hector. "Are you alright?"

She most certainly was not, but after a moment more of struggling, she cleared her throat.

"Yes," she said softly. "It's just that I was hoping to speak to Paris."

If she could only speak with him alone. He, of all people, knew it was possible to be so favored by the gods they would involve humans in their immortal affairs. She and Paris had both experienced this, had they not? And in the end, they had both been cursed.

She had lost all power of persuasion and Paris had lost all reason.

"Alone," she said, glancing at her father for permission. "If I may."

"There is no need for that, Cassandra," said Paris, causing her head to whip around in his direction. To her horror, Apollo stood behind her brother, shimmering like a mirage. "I'm sure whatever you want to say can be said in front of us all. In fact, I prefer it."

Cassandra's fingers went numb, and she could do nothing to stop her grip on the wine jug from loosening, just as she could not stop the rant she knew was coming.

"You can't go," she whispered, knowing it was the quiet before the storm.

"I must," replied Paris, staring at her with an intensity to match hers. Did he know what she'd seen? That she knew everything?

"Then Troy will burn," she shot back. "I have seen it."

Paris tilted his head and smiled.

"You have it wrong, sister," he said. "I go so Troy will *not* burn."

"Lies!" shrieked Cassandra. The crash of clay against stone barely registered. All she heard was the thrumming in her ears. "I know why you go, what you were promised," she spat out. "And we will all burn for it!"

She'd intended to speak more calmly, with reason, but she was not of her own volition anymore. She ran through the broken shards of clay over to Priam, falling to her knees before him.

"Please, father," she begged, her words coming out in a jumbled mess as she grabbed for the bottom of his tunic. "Fire! I have seen it. Don't let him go. You must believe me. Everyone... burning... I have *seen* it!"

"Enough of your nonsense, girl!" yelled Priam. Thoroughly enraged, he pulled the pristine white fabric from her grasp with a snap. "Guards!"

The door flew open, cracking loudly against the stone walls as the guards burst into the room. Hector had jumped from his chair, gently prying Cassandra away from Priam before the guards got their hands on her.

"Hector, please," said Cassandra through a torrent of tears, letting go of Priam's robe to clutch the collar of Hector's tunic. "I speak truth. You believe me, don't you?"

"Shhh," said Hector, guiding her to her feet and taking her into his embrace. He'd always had a soft spot for her. "Quiet now, Cassandra. Paris and I will be fine. There is no need to work yourself into a frenzy, little sister."

Cassandra sobbed. He did not believe her. No one did. They thought her mad, and they would rather lock her away than listen.

A scream swelled in her throat when she finally realized why. Apollo had cursed her to tell the truth, but never be believed. She bit back a scream. Oh, how she despised him for doing this to her. But he would not break her, for she would never stop trying to prevent the destruction of her beloved homeland.

"If you and Paris goes to Sparta, Troy will be no more," she said, praying beyond hope her brothers would heed her warning.

"Take her to her room and see that she stays there until I say otherwise," said Priam, dismissing her with a hard tap of his staff to the floor.

Rough hands grabbed Cassandra by the arms, pulling her from Hector. Cassandra fought against them, kicking and screaming as the same guards who had let her in dragged her away.

CHAPTER 7

CASSANDRA STARED AT the plate of moldy bread, watching the flies crawl along its surface before clutching her stomach and trying not to retch. She'd told the handmaid to stop bringing food to her room, but the woman hadn't listened.

Cassandra laughed out loud at the irony.

She'd just settled down in a chair next to the hearth when there came a knock at the door, startling her. Although she'd had none so far, she was allowed visitors; it was she who could not leave. The handmaiden Hecuba had assigned to Cassandra had stopped knocking after the first few days of her confinement. Now the woman came and went as she pleased, bringing Cassandra food she refused to eat, but mostly to make sure she hadn't ripped more hair from her head or scratched her own eyes out.

Whomever was knocking must be her first visitor. As if divining her thoughts, a muffled voice came from the other side of the heavy door.

"Cassandra? Cassandra, it's me, Helenus. Can I come in?"

Cassandra snickered. How gracious of him to ask. It had only taken two weeks for him to come. She sighed. Despite her resentment he hadn't come to visit her sooner, she supposed she should be thankful he had come at all.

"Come in," said Cassandra, suddenly glad for the company. Had she been trapped in her room for two weeks or two years? Perhaps he had come bearing the good news that her imprisonment was over.

The door swung open, and she turned her head when she heard Helenus's shuffling footsteps come to an abrupt stop.

"You look terrible," he said.

Had it not been true, Cassandra would have berated him for the insult. But she had not allowed herself any pampering afforded to a princess, instead choosing to sit and wallow in her misery on principle.

"I feel terrible," she replied, noticing the small bowl of fresh ripe figs in his hands. Hunger stabbed at her belly, unleashing a long, low growl that betrayed her resolve.

"Here, eat these," he said, handing her the bowl.

Even though she was still irritated with him, she reached for it. She was famished, and at least he was here now.

She set the bowl of fruit in her lap while he pulled over a chair to sit opposite her. She waited until he was settled and staring at her before selecting the biggest fig.

"I'm not a lunatic," she said before biting into it, her stomach rumbling in both anticipation and gratitude. "You know I see things, Helenus, and you know what I say is true."

Helenus raked his fingers through his hair. "I know that, but only because I have seen things, too."

"Because of me," replied Cassandra, taking another bite of fig.

She resisted the urge to move it out of his reach when Helenus leaned forward to select a fig from the bowl. Was there ever a time he wasn't eating? There were more than enough to share, of course, but she was a bit possessive of the fruit now that she remembered how good it tasted.

"Because of you?" Helenus bit into a fig, furrowing his brow as he chewed. "I thought we got it from—"

"Once," cut in Cassandra. She swallowed a mouthful of fig before continuing. "Mother saw something *once*, and it was a dream, not a vision. She is no seer, not like Aesacus, me, or you."

"So, who gave us this gift, then?" asked Helenus.

"I've already told you," Cassandra said flatly. "The god of prophecy." She resisted the urge to roll her eyes. He could be watching, waiting for her to slight him again so he could inflict even more woe upon her.

"Apollo?" asked Helenus.

He sighed wearily when she nodded, just like everyone else who thought she was merely seeking attention. Irritation spiked through her, and she glared at him.

"Why are you here, Helenus?"

"Cassandra..." he replied. "I think our brother's return has been the hardest on you. Before Troy found out it had another prince, we—*you*—were the apple of our father's eye."

Apple? Was he trying to say that he'd seen visions of the goddesses, too?

"This is not about trying to get attention from father," said Cassandra. "I am not some spoiled princess jealous of her long-lost brother's homecoming. As I have told you all,

Troy will burn if Paris goes to Sparta. I have seen it."

"This is what I've come to tell you," said Helenus, his voice laced with concern. "You say Troy will burn but cannot say how or when or why. To them, you speak nonsense."

"Then help me, Helenus," she said. "Help me make them understand."

"It's too late, sister. Paris and Hector have left for Sparta. They should have arrived two days ago."

Cassandra closed her eyes, expecting to see flames and destruction. All she saw was Paris, cupping the woman's face, their lips mere inches apart.

"He betrays us all..." The edges of her vision went black, the scene blurring into nothing more than swirling colors and shapes. "With one kiss he..."

"This is why we are all worried about you," said Helenus, gently shaking her out of her stupor.

"It is because I have been cursed!" yelled Cassandra, shoving him away. "To speak the truth but never be believed. No one is listening, not even you, Helenus. That is why you are all hearing nonsense!"

Helenus stared at her, waiting for further explanation. Gods save her, why could she not open her mouth without the words that left it turning into an incoherent rant.

"He came to me and..." she began, her gaze going to the banked embers in the hearth because she was unable to look her brother in the eye. How could she put it delicately? "I refused him."

"I believe you, Cassandra," said Helenus.

He didn't look at her when he said it, and she knew him well enough to know that he was placating her.

"What, exactly, do you believe, Helenus?"

"That father locking you away is doing more harm than good," said Helenus. "Now, come. Let us go for a walk in the fresh air."

Cassandra sighed, out of relief or frustration she did not know, but she reached out and took her brother's hand. She could not fault him for trying to help. He did not know her fate; whether she roamed the grounds or wasted away in her room, she would never be free from Apollo's curse.

CHAPTER 8

CASSANDRA SHIVERED AS she set the piece of papyrus down, her fingers trembling as she lit the incense. Finally managing to coax a flame to catch, she blew it out, watching the smoke rise while she listened to the cicadas sing their song. True, it was the dead of night, and it was only a stone likeness she knelt before, but she hadn't wanted to wait one moment longer to take matters into her own hands.

She would ask Apollo to lift his curse.

Cassandra had thought about coming during the day but decided against it. The temple would have been too crowded. Sacrificing a swan when there was no holy day would also garner suspicion. Besides, she had tried to get her hands on one, to make her appeal for forgiveness more enticing, but it'd been a futile endeavor. The keen eyes of palace servants had been watching her every move for weeks. She had done well acting like her old self, pretending and smiling at them all, but they were still afraid she would break out into one of her fits.

She'd been lucky enough to slip away to the temple unnoticed, which would not have been the case had she tried to carry a protesting swan to sacrifice. Offering a poem and lighting incense in Apollo's honor was the best she could do under her unfortunate circumstances.

She looked up at the statue. Its features were pleasing, but it looked nothing like Apollo, and she didn't know whether to laugh or cry that she knew so much about the god the others did not.

Like how cruel he could be if he did not get his way.

After bending at the waist and placing her forehead on the cold stone floor, she said, "I beseech you, Apollo. Come to me. I will sing. I will dance. I will ask for your mercy until I can no longer speak. I will do whatever it takes to be rid of this wretched curse you have placed upon me."

She repeated her summons over and over, laying prostrate for hours begging for Apollo to come, but it was to no avail. He would not oblige, and her prayers would go unanswered.

Exhaustion finally overtook Cassandra, her fervent pleas turning to incoherent mumbling. She must get back to the palace before dawn, and so she stirred, beginning the process of unfolding her limbs and dragging herself to her feet. Once standing, she made her way toward the door on numb and prickling legs.

"Leaving so soon?"

Cassandra whirled around, quick as a striking snake.

There he stood, flesh and bone leaning cross-armed against his own statue.

"Where's my dance?" asked Apollo.

Cassandra shielded her eyes, blinking against the golden light of the sunrise suddenly flooding the temple. Of course, he would wait until daybreak to come.

"You said you'd do anything, Cassandra. Or are you still a liar?"

"If I dance, you will lift the curse?"

"There is no guarantee it will suffice." Apollo shrugged. "But I will consider it."

Cassandra stared at him, knowing full well he only sought to humiliate her. Anger flared her nostrils, and no matter how hard she tried, she could not stop her lip from curling.

"Why do you do this?" There was so much more she wanted to say, so many more questions she wanted to ask, but she knew it was no use. She had been Apollo's object of desire from the very start. And now, since she'd had the audacity to deny him what he thought

58

he was entitled to, she was the target of his revenge. If he could not satisfy his lust for her, he would take pleasure in holding his grudge against her for the rest of her life.

"Because I can," he replied, proving her theory correct. "I gave you so much and asked for so little. Now..." He unfolded his arms to twirl a finger at her. "Show me how sorry you are."

Cassandra's feet moved on their own, shuffling her around in circles. She let out a cry of alarm when her arms flailed wildly at the behest of the god who once favored her. Tears streamed down her face as he forced her to bend to his will.

How long she went on this way, Apollo's laughter ringing in her ears as she danced round and round his statue, she did not know. Hours? Days? Weeks? She only knew she gasped when she saw the horrified man standing at the top of the temple steps, shards of the clay jar he'd been holding shattered on the ground around him.

She stood there, panting and sweating, hair and dress akimbo. Neither of them spoke. She only blinked at him as he stared wide-eyed at her. When she realized he thought it had been *her* who'd been laughing maniacally, she crumpled to the floor and began to wail.

The man backed away slowly, feeling for the edge of the stair with his foot.

"Help me," croaked Cassandra, her throat suddenly dry as a bone. She reached for the man, convulsing as she crawled toward him.

"There is no help for you, princess," said the man before turning and fleeing in terror.

Cassandra laid her burning cheek on the cool stone floor and wept, defeated in the knowledge she would never wake up from her living nightmare.

CHAPTER 9

CASSANDRA STOOD ON the balcony next to her mother, trying not to shiver as she watched the longship carrying Paris and Hector back to Troy sail into the harbor. Though six months had passed, her mother remained stoic, expertly concealing her excitement for the long-awaited return of her sons.

Cassandra, however, openly trembled in fear. Oh, how she hoped Paris stepped off that boat alone.

She tore her gaze away from the billowing sails to peer down at her father and brothers waiting in the courtyard below. Hecuba, too, must have seen how they craned their necks and stamped their feet. She inhaled deeply before turning toward Cassandra, giving her a look.

It was a silent command that said, "Cause no trouble," and Cassandra swallowed hard before nodding, determined to try. With a whoosh of expensive fabric and the jangle of fine jewelry, Hecuba left to go meet her eldest sons at the shore and welcome them home.

Cassandra followed behind her mother in silence as they made their way down to the city streets. All of Troy had come out to witness the return of their princes, beloved Hector and adored Paris, and when the royal procession passed through the gates, they fell in behind Cassandra and Helenus, who followed behind Deiphobus.

The crowd gathered around a platform. It had been erected so their king and queen could sit, waiting in comfort as the *trireme* docked. Priam and Hecuba took their place, while Cassandra went to stand next to Helenus.

He smiled at her, excited to reunite with their eldest brothers. Cassandra managed to pretend she, too, was happy, but her insides roiled without mercy. She threaded her arm through her twin's elbow and waited for Hector and Paris to disembark.

The cold wind whipped the loose strands of her hair and stung her eyes, but her head was blessedly clear. She heard the roar of the waves, but not the thrumming that accompanied her visions, and she took it to be a good sign.

When the ship finally reached the dock, men peeled and dropped onto the wooden platform like leeches burned by the heat of a flame. The oars were drawn in, crewmen in the riggings threw down ropes, and before long the ship was secured.

Hector came down the ramp first, waving to the cheering crowd. Overjoyed to see Hector alive and well, Cassandra unthreaded her arm from Helenus and joined in the clapping.

Her heart pounded in her chest when she noticed Hector's smile did not reach his eyes.

She held her breath, not intending for her teeth to slice through flesh but tasting blood, nonetheless. If Paris returned home without the woman, the prophecy she had seen would not be fulfilled. Troy would not be doomed, not while Priam ruled, anyway.

Paris appeared next, pausing at the top of the ramp to soak in the applause. Cassandra exhaled, relieved to see him standing there alone.

And then she saw it.

He held something; it was a woman's hand.

Cassandra could not move, could not speak... Could not breathe.

Shouts of joy turned into confused murmurs as Paris made his way down the plank with a golden-haired beauty in tow.

Priam rose from his chair, Hecuba from hers. All eyes, including Cassandra's, turned to

Hector, who stood before them with his hands clasped in front of him, braced for the barrage of questions that would surely be directed his way.

"Hector?" asked Priam. "What is the meaning of this?"

"She was stowed away," replied Hector. He glanced at Paris and the woman walking toward them hand in hand before continuing. "I did not know she was on the ship until we left Sparta."

"Who is she?" asked Hecuba.

Hector pressed his lips thin, closing his eyes for a moment before revealing her identity. "Helen."

"Wife of Menelaus?" said Priam, sounding alarmed.

He very well should be, thought Cassandra as she leaned into Helenus for support, straining to hear the rest of the conversation over the pounding in her ears.

"Take her back," she whispered, bile rising in her throat.

Helenus gripped her arm painfully. "Shhh."

It seemed he was engrossed in the conversation as well, though judging by the stunned expression on his face, enthralled was a better way to put it. Disgusted at her brother's blatant admiration of the woman approaching alongside Paris, Cassandra let go of Helenus, stiffening her back and lifting her chin when Paris and Helen finally reached the dais.

Priam wasted no time on pleasantries. "Paris?"

"Father, mother," he replied, nodding at each of them in turn. "This is my wife, Helen."

Helen nodded politely, and Cassandra wondered if she was smiling demurely behind her veil or smirking viciously.

"So we've been informed." Priam looked at Helen but did not say a word.

"Paris, you married another man's wife?" asked Hecuba.

Paris smiled broadly. "It was the goddess Aphrodite's will, mother." He turned and looked at the woman next to him with love struck eyes. "And who dare go against the will of Olympus? Not Agelaus, and certainly not I." He caressed Helen's cheek, as if the destruction of them all had not been set in motion.

Cassandra wanted to pummel him with her fists.

She was relieved, however, when her father was not convinced it was nothing more than lust that had landed Helen on his shores.

"She must be returned to Sparta," he said, shaking his head at Hector. "You should have changed course at once."

"Come now, father, don't blame Hector," said Paris. "He is a good man and a better brother. He did not know we eloped, and when he discovered we had, he could not, in good conscience, separate me from my wife."

Persuaded by his silver tongue and handsome face, the crowd nodded their heads, murmuring their assent and causing Cassandra to grind her teeth. Could Paris do no wrong? He tells them it's the will of the gods and they *believe* him?

Cassandra clutched the ends of her hair and pulled, horrified to see Hecuba's hard demeanor soften like clay in Paris's hands. Helpless, she could do nothing but groan when her mother turned toward her father with a pleading heart.

"If she makes our son happy, perhaps we should not be so quick to judge."

Priam inhaled, nodding so slightly Cassandra clung to the hope this day, the one they had all been waiting months for, was a dream. Reality shattered any hope her father had given her a moment later when Hecuba stepped forward and took Paris's hands in hers.

"Welcome home, my son." Her watery eyes were as full of love as her heart, and every mother in the crowd bit back a sob when their queen turned to Helen and said, "Welcome to Troy." Hecuba turned and faced the crowd. "Tonight, we offer Apollo a hecatomb for the safe return of Hector and Paris."

Cassandra's temples pounded, and she whimpered with the effort not to retch. It took all the will she had to fight the urge to charge forward and push Helen back onto the boat.

Why hadn't she just given in to Apollo's advances? Perhaps then none of this would be happening.

With their mother, father, and Hector heading through the parted crowd and back up to the palace, Helenus jumped at the chance to speak with Paris.

"Congratulations, brother," said Helenus, clasping forearms with Paris. When he turned to address his brother's wife, the color in his cheeks deepened. "Welcome, Helen of Troy."

Helen of *Troy*?

Cassandra could take no more. She dug her fingers into Helenus's arm and yanked him out of the way.

"Go back to Sparta," she spat. Helen had taken too much from her already. She'd be damned if she would allow the wily woman to ensnare Helenus as well.

Helen's eyes widened, and Cassandra wanted to slap her hard across the face. No, she wanted to rip her limb from limb. This woman, this treacherous *Achaean,* had broken her vows to one man to run away with another, and she dared look surprised to be met with hostility?

"Cassandra," scolded Paris, stepping between her and his new wife. "That is not how Troy welcomes its newest princess."

Even though she barely knew Paris, his reprimand still stung. Jaw set and nostrils flaring, Cassandra dug down deep to muster the strength to remain both still and quiet.

"Come, my love," said Paris, turning his attention back to Helen. "Let us go meet your new people."

With that, they walked away, leaving Cassandra fuming where she stood. Helenus glanced at her before shaking his head and following the couple back to the palace.

Disapproving whispers filled her ears, and the narrow-eyed glares pressing in on her dredged mortified tears to the rims of her eyes. She hurried to catch up, staring daggers into the back of Paris's and Helen's heads, wishing she had real knives in her grip. She knew what was coming next, and her stomach turned once they passed through the gate.

Cassandra clutched her belly with one hand, the other clamping over her mouth when, after stepping through the gates of Troy, Paris turned toward Helen and bent down to kiss her.

CHAPTER 10

CASSANDRA STARED INTO the flames transfixed, barely hearing the sizzle of the spitted thighs as they dropped their fat onto the hot coals. The smell of smoke and roasting meat was overwhelming, yet she dared herself to move closer. She wanted to know what it would feel like when her body caught fire.

Unable to stand the searing heat for more than a few moments, she stepped back with a defeated huff and retreated into the coolness of the night air.

The sounds of celebration swirled around the courtyard. People feasted and drank, spilling their cups as they danced to the lyres and the drums. It made Cassandra sick with unease, but what could she do? Twice now she had tried to warn these people. It was bad enough her entire family had accepted their fate so easily, but the whole city was enamored with their newest prince and princess, even if she did tell them what was coming, they would not believe her.

The thought of Apollo's kiss came unbidden to her mind, the way he had forced it upon her, and she spat the memory into the fire. As if her act of defiance had conjured him, when she looked up, she saw his face staring back at her from the other side of the flames.

"What are you doing here?" she hissed, no longer concerned with keeping her facade of normalcy. Let them think she was insane.

The corners of Apollo's lips tipped upward. "I've come to make peace with you."

She tilted her head. Something was wrong. The smile, it was too gentle, and he did not speak with his own voice, but in a woman's higher pitch and timber.

Cassandra blinked, brows knitting in confusion. Would he ever stop playing such trickery on her?

The burning wood popped before falling in on itself, sending a curtain of glowing embers into the night sky. When they faded, it was not Apollo, but Helen who looked back at her.

Cassandra gasped, her mouth dropping open in surprise. Recovering quickly, she clamped it shut before turning to leave.

"Please, hear me out," said Helen.

Cassandra stopped. She had seen flashes of Troy's harbor filled with Grecian war ships. She'd said nothing because no one was listening, but if Cassandra kept the raving madwoman that sometimes possessed her at bay, perhaps Helen would.

If she could keep her wits and composure in check, and not scream obscenities at the woman, there might be a chance. If she could make Helen understand what she and Paris had done, perhaps she would go back on her own, before it was too late.

"Why have you come here?" asked Cassandra.

"That is what I've come to talk to you about," replied Helen, "However, judging by your cold reception of our arrival this morning, I'm not sure you will ever believe the truth."

Cassandra snorted at the irony. "I was happy for my brothers' arrival, Helen. Not yours."

Helen sighed. "Have you ever been in love, Cassandra?"

There may have been a chance for that once, but it had been selfishly snatched away.

"No."

Helen nodded, as though she'd expected this answer. "Do you think I married Menelaus because I wanted to?" She shook her head. "I am only a pawn in their quest for power, Cassandra. We all are."

Cassandra resisted the urge to roll her eyes. "Tell me, Helen of Sparta, how is it that a woman would give up a kingdom for a man she has only just met?" Cassandra balled her hands into fists, welcoming the pain of her nails biting into her palms.

"Do you think Sparta was mine to rule?"

Cassandra knew the answer but refused to say it out loud. She would not give Helen the satisfaction of being right.

"There is no other way to explain it than we are fated," continued Helen. "From the moment I saw Paris, his heart called to mine. He desires *me*, not what he could gain from my father. Paris does not wish to rule a kingdom, his only ambition is to love me, wholly and completely, a rarity among men."

Cassandra cringed, unable to tolerate Helen's talk of fate a moment longer. This was not some fanciful notion of love and desire. It was a matter of life and death. What would it take for this woman to see she wasn't simply a pawn of Menelaus to achieve power and glory? It was much worse than that. She and Paris were puppets in the games the *gods* played, and the death and destruction from the web in which they had been caught would be more immense than Helen could even fathom.

Cassandra gathered her skirts and made her way around the fire pit as calmly as she could manage, willing herself to approach slowly.

"It is bigger than that, Helen," she said, placing one foot in front of the other carefully. "Do you not find it curious that not only do you profess your love so quickly, but you agree to become another man's wife knowing it will cause a war?" She cocked her head slowly, avoiding any sudden movement. "Don't you see? It is the work of the gods. Aphrodite... Apollo... even Zeus. Menelaus nor Agamemnon will sit by idly. They will come for you. So, I ask you again, why have you come here?"

"Troy is strong," replied Helen, taking a step back. Her voice trembled. "Paris has assured me its walls will hold."

Cassandra continued her advance. She had no idea what she would do once she reached Helen, but she could not stop despite the awful thrumming now filling her head.

"He loves me, and I love him," whispered Helen.

Helen's words were the last thing Cassandra heard before the low hum turned into a driving and relentless *dah-dum, dah-dum, dah-dum* that grew louder with every step. She saw Helen's horrified expression between flashes of hooves striking the ground.

"Cassandra!" said Paris. "That's quite enough."

Pulled out of her trance, she stumbled to a stop. She blinked, and both the vision and the thrumming disappeared, replaced by the loud pop and crackle of dancing flames.

"Helen is my wife," said Paris, offering his hand and continuing only when Helen took it. "She is here to stay, sister, and it will do you well to make peace with it."

Cassandra glared at Paris, trying to find it in her heart to forgive the man—her own brother—who had doomed Troy.

She could not.

All she could do now was accept her own fate.

"Well, then, congratulations," said Cassandra. "May you remain in the favor of the gods."

CHAPTER 11

One year later

CASSANDRA STIFLED A yawn, silently thanking Hera it wasn't *her* marriage Hecuba was finalizing. Hair and eyes dark as midnight, Andromache, princess of Anatolia, sat across from the women of Troy with her similarly dark-featured *kyrios*, the guardian responsible with delivering her dowry. Chests of gold, expensive fabric, and spools of fine wool lay open between them. Hecuba took her time inspecting their contents, but when she finally finished, it was decided that Andromache was officially betrothed to Hector.

There wasn't much choice in the matter. He had gone to Anatolia after the death of her mother, who had succumbed to illness. It was rumored losing her husband Eetion and several of her sons during a sack of Anatolia by the Greeks was the real reason for her death.

"We will wait for *Gamelion* for the *Gamos*," said Hecuba.

Andromache's *kyrios* nodded in agreement. "Yes, the wedding season is the best time to hold the ceremonies."

Cassandra looked at Helen pointedly. This was the right way to marry, but of course, Helen refused to look at her.

Although life went on in the many months since Helen had forced herself upon the people of Troy, Cassandra did not grow to like her, only to tolerate her. At times like this, when Paris was not around to protect her, Cassandra couldn't resist the temptation to remind her sister-in-law just how much her presence was unwanted.

By Cassandra, at least.

"There is no sense in going back to Anatolia. You both shall stay in Troy. Our people will want to get to know the woman who is to become Hector's wife." Andromache had gone pale as milk, and so Hecuba added, "We are sorry for your loss, Andromache. Eetion was a good man, your mother faithful and devout. Troy welcomes you with open arms."

Andromache offered them all a weak smile.

"Thank you, *Anassa*," said the man who's name Cassandra had already forgotten. "Words cannot express our gratitude, especially to

Hector. He is an honorable and chivalrous man."

Cassandra's stomach looped, shocked when she saw the tears well in Andromache's eyes. Andromache wasn't prone to displaying such emotion, not publicly, at least.

The rescue of the princess of Anatolia by the heir of Troy had been no surprise. Anatolia and Troy had always been allies, with Andromache and her brothers visiting the city several times. It was no secret Hector had grown fond of Andromache over the years, but Cassandra supposed that didn't mean his warrior heart would allow Andromache's strong will—her name meant "fighter of men," after all—a place in their marriage. They had bantered often as children, but that did not mean they would not bicker as adults.

Even though Cassandra couldn't imagine what it was like for Andromache to lose her entire family, then have your childhood friend save you from being an invading Greek's wife, she could image the fear and worry of having to change who you are out of debt. It was a heavy weight, and Cassandra knew the tears in Andromache's eyes were from the hope Hector would continue to find her independence a comfort instead of a threat.

The *kyrios* cleared his throat, scattering Cassandra's thoughts.

"You are well matched, Andromache," he said, nodding at her reassuringly. He turned his dark eyes to Hecuba. "It has been my pleasure to present the dowry, Your Highness, but I'm sure you have much to discuss with your soon-to-be daughter-in-law. If you will please excuse me."

Hecuba nodded and the man stood. He was old enough to be Andromache's father and was no doubt a relative or some trusted friend of the family. He must have been, decided Cassandra, for he looked at the princess with the care and concern for a child known since birth.

Jealousy nipped at her as she watched the man leave. What that must be like, to be shown such affection.

"Helen, please see that Andromache has all she needs," said Hecuba, drawing Cassandra's attention back to the women. "I must speak with Cassandra alone."

A burst of adrenaline pulsed through Cassandra at the same time the ever-obedient Helen nodded. Dismissed, Helen and Andromache hurried out of the room, the gauzy trains of their dresses floating behind them like clouds blown by a strong wind.

Hecuba inhaled deeply, steeling herself. Ever since the return of Paris, and especially after the arrival of Helen, she always did this when speaking to Cassandra. It was as if she were being forced to perform a task that brought her great displeasure.

Cassandra dropped her gaze to her lap and waited for the criticisms to begin. She didn't understand how there could be so many, especially when she no longer spoke of what she saw. Blessedly, there hadn't even been a need; she hadn't had a vision in months.

"Your father and I have agreed to the betrothal of you and Euryplyus, son of Telephus."

"Of Mysia?" replied Cassandra.

"Yes. It is time for you to marry."

She could feel her impertinence bubbling in the pit of her stomach, rising to her chest, and funneling into her throat. It tasted like ash when it gathered on her tongue and spewed from her mouth. "Why would anyone agree to wed their son to a woman who spoke nothing but nonsense?"

"Govern yourself. This may be the only chance for marriage you have left."

"This is not for my benefit, mother," replied Cassandra, trying to keep the smugness from her voice. "The backing of a powerful allied army is for Troy's benefit."

Even if they insisted on calling her prophecies nothing more than the rantings of a maniacal lunatic, it was evident that, on some level, Priam and Hecuba felt the need to align themselves with a kingdom that would join a fight against the *Achaeans*. What better way to ensure an obligation than to wed her to its heir?

"You know they are coming, don't you? You feel it in your bones. They come for Helen, amassing their war ships as we speak." Then, seeing her chance to rid her city of the woman for whom a thousand ships would launch, she added, "Not that you do, of course, but if you *were* to believe what I say to be true, wouldn't it be wise to send Helen of *Sparta* away while you still can?"

A muscle in Hecuba's jaw ticked over her clenched teeth. "Troy is impenetrable."

"Ha!" shouted Cassandra, springing to her feet. "You admit you fear they come to take back what is theirs, then." Her mother leaned back when Cassandra stepped toward her. She hadn't meant the action to be menacing, only to get close enough so that her mother could hear her next words very clearly.

"Marry me to whomever you wish," laughed Cassandra. "It will not matter in the end."

Hecuba's hand shot out, slapping her hard across the face.

Cassandra recoiled but did not retreat, nor did she reach up to soothe her stinging cheek. Instead, she inhaled deeply as she straightened, steeling herself much like her mother had at the beginning of their conversation.

"Have it your way." The words came out in an exhausted rasp. She was beyond tired of this curse. She shrugged, utterly defeated. "I know nothing."

CHAPTER 12

Three years later

CASSANDRA HAD NOT been surprised when the first Grecian ship had been spotted on the horizon, nor did she panic when the horns had begun to blare their alarm. In fact, she'd found it amusing the way the servants had darted about, frantic, as though they were poultry desperately trying to escape the snapping jaws of a fox.

Her mother had ordered them to remain calm, which had been absurd. So much so, it had made her want to laugh out loud, and so she had. The one thing she hadn't dared do, however, was gloat about how the marriage negotiations had been abandoned when the Greeks, spilling onto the beach like ants, took control of the harbor, even though she'd felt the spiteful words on the tip of her tongue.

That, she had decided, would only push her mother to inflict an even harsher blow than a slap to the face. The pain she had already suffered was too great.

Even now, after three years of fighting, no one acknowledged Cassandra's prediction that Menelaus would come for Helen had indeed come to pass. Thanks to cunning Odysseus, the rest of Helen's suitors swore an oath several years earlier, forcing them to put aside their differences to fight alongside him and his brother Agamemnon to honor it. Even Achilles, the greatest warrior among them, had been persuaded to join in. He alone brought fifty ships full of Myrmidons.

Sometimes Cassandra would watch the fighting from atop the palace. She could always tell when Achilles was on the battlefield. His golden armor flashed under the sun and his terrifying war cry carried on the wind for miles.

She couldn't see the famed warrior's features from the battlements, but in her mind's eye, she saw clearly how he bared his perfect white teeth as he thrust his spear in the chests of Trojan soldiers. But she also knew that Priam was a powerful king and Hector a shrewd general. If they had kept the Greeks at bay for this long, who's to say this war could not come to an end, with a peaceful resolution instead of more bloodshed.

If only Paris would hand over Helen.

To keep her mind off the uncertainty of it all, she often sat at the loom, as she did now, or pretended to learn some other chore. She admitted it seemed pointless at times—she may never get the chance to run a household—but what else was there to do?

Cassandra stopped her weaving to stretch her sore limbs. Andromache, heavily pregnant, did the same.

"You should eat something, Cassandra," said Andromache, supporting the bottom of her belly as she rose from her stool. She waddled over to Cassandra and laid a hand on her shoulder. "It's been days."

"I will," said Cassandra, turning herself around. "But first I must talk to Astyanax."

Andromache tilted her head, and Cassandra smiled up at the gentle reproach before placing her hands on either side of her beloved sister-in-law's belly. Andromache was going to make an excellent mother. Had it been Hecuba, there would have been no discussion, only command.

"His name is Scamandrius," sighed Andromache.

"I know," replied Cassandra, "but being called *High King* sounds much better than being named after a dirty old river."

Andromache laughed. "With as much as you dote on him already, he will be born thinking he has two mothers."

Cassandra leaned in close and whispered, "Hello Astyanax. Are you awake? It is your *theia*, Cassandra."

She laid her ear on Andromache's stomach and listened. She could not help but smile when she heard the faint sound of a tiny heartbeat. She could not wait for Astyanax to be born. He would be the best of Hector and Andromache, and the pride and joy of Troy.

Cassandra closed her eyes, content to listen to the precious beating forever, but when it grew louder, her brow furrowed. The noise filled her head with a steady thrumming, and her eyes popped open when it became a heavy pounding. This could not be right. She lifted her head slightly, to gauge whether the sound was coming from the baby's heart or from inside her head. The pounding filled her ears. She sat frozen in terror, waiting for another vision to roll her eyes into the back of her head.

First, she saw nothing but black, but then she saw blood on stone.

Cassandra's starved and scrawny arms reached for Andromache's waist.

Next, she saw a baby boy, with the chestnut curls of his father, laying broken where he had landed.

She pulled Andromache closer, as though it would keep the tears from bursting from her eyes.

"Cassandra?" said Andromache. "What is it?"

Cassandra inhaled a shaky breath. She would not tell Andromache. The woman was strong, but the loss of a child in such a way would break any mother. Cassandra would find a way to save her nephew.

"You know me well," said Cassandra sitting back to wipe away her tears with the heel of her hand. "I should eat something."

Andromache pulled Cassandra to her feet. "Astyanax and I will join you."

Her stomach felt sour, and food was the last thing on her mind, but Cassandra didn't want to disappoint Andromache. She tried blocking out the horror she'd seen as they walked down the corridor.

"Do you think the war will end soon?" said Cassandra. It was a desperate attempt to keep her mind from replaying the tragic scene.

"Yes, I do believe it will all be over soon." Andromache rested a protective hand on her belly. "If anyone can save us, it will be Hector."

Cassandra cringed. It wasn't up to Hector. More Olympians had gotten involved now—Zeus, Hera, Athena, even Ares—and they had all chosen sides. This was as much a divine battle as it was a mortal one. Cassandra was surprised Paris hadn't taken Helen to Memphis years ago, to wait out the war in safety at the palace of King Proteus of Egypt.

"Why won't Paris give her back?" murmured Cassandra. It was a rhetorical question, but Andromache took it as quizzical.

"Love is a powerful force." Andromache shook her head, at a loss for a more concrete explanation. "Hector risked his life for it."

Cassandra couldn't disagree. Aphrodite was a powerful goddess. Dolling out love and lust however she saw fit. In the case of Hector, she had bestowed love. Paris, however, was overcome with lust. It was the reason why he and Helen both turned a blind eye to the death and destruction happening all around them. How else was it possible for Helen to abandon her child?

"Oh," grunted Andromache, pressing on her belly. She reached for Cassandra's hand and placed it on the tiny foot-shaped bulge that appeared. The baby's kick was strong and Andromache's smile wide. "A warrior like his father."

Weak as it was, Cassandra offered a cheerful grin even though her revelation was profound and her sadness great.

CHAPTER 13

Six years later

CASSANDRA SHIVERED, WRAPPING her arms tighter around her middle as she looked on from the battlements. Paris was addressing Menelaus, and it looked as though a truce had been called, with each side laying down their weapons as the two men talked. She assumed they were discussing settling their differences with one-on-one combat. Why had they not done this ten years ago? Cassandra didn't know, but she supposed the gods had something to do with it.

Both would always find a reason to war with each other.

A messenger had been sent into the palace with word of the duel, and the women had rushed to the battlements so they could watch from a safe distance. Cassandra secretly rooted for Menelaus. She did not wish to see Paris die, but if it meant the war would be over, and Menelaus would take Helen back to Sparta, then so be it.

Astyanax pointed at the men gathered down on the plain outside the wall, to one man, in particular. "Pappa," he said, bouncing in Andromache's arms and squealing with delight.

"Yes, Astyanax," Andromache stroked her son's soft curls as she kissed his temple. "That is your *pappa*, and he will protect us."

Cassandra's stomach dropped. They could not see what she saw; a woman dressed in a flowing white *chiton*, cinched with a gleaming girdle. Her golden hair shined bright like the rosy dawn, and she towered over the tallest man. Cassandra knew it was Aphrodite who stood on the sidelines, drawn to the duel out of concern for Paris.

Cassandra sighed, despair settling in her bones. If Aphrodite championed him, this war would continue.

As if summoned by her misery, Cassandra heard the voice of Apollo echo in her head.

What a curious situation, wouldn't you agree?

"Why do you torment me?" she whispered, low and harsh, not surprised he would come to taunt her at such a pivotal moment.

Hecuba and Andromache's heads snapped from the drama below to her. Hecuba's eyes narrowed, and Cassandra bit her lip to stop anymore words from escaping.

How curious... A shepherd thinking he can outfight a hardened soldier.

The clang of metal, faint as it was, drew her gaze to the two men lunging at each other with swords.

Who do you suppose convinced Paris he could best Menelaus?

Her heart raced when she heard the grunt of pain as Menelaus's sword crashed down hard upon Paris's bronze helmet.

Was it Hermes?

Cassandra gasped when Menelaus's sword broke in half, the blade ricocheting off Paris's cracked helmet and landing in the dirt. Menelaus bellowed in frustration, screaming words at the sky Cassandra could not understand.

Zeus?

She clenched her fists at her side as she watched Paris try and scramble to his feet when Menelaus stormed toward him.

Or was it I?

Her teeth tore through the inside of her cheek when the Greek king dragged Paris back into the center of the makeshift fighting ring by the strap of his helmet.

With a wave of Aphrodite's hand, the strap broke, freeing Paris from Menelaus's enraged grip. Paris scurried backward, and Cassandra's lungs seized when a white mist rose from the ground to obscure him. The fog billowed upward, and when it was gone, so was Paris.

The men on both sides shot to their feet. Dazed, their heads swiveling this way and that, looking for Paris. But he was nowhere to be found, and so they eyed each other in mutual confusion.

Cassandra flinched when a bright light suddenly flashed between the armies.

Ah, it was only a matter of time before Athena got involved. She despises Troy...

"Stop," cried Cassandra, covering her ears as though the voice in her head would cease.

She moaned, not caring about the stern look from Hecuba her outburst had surely garnered, or the concerned expression that must be on Andromache's face.

With Apollo quieted, Cassandra uncovered her ears to grip the edge of the stone wall. She looked on in anticipation at the men, thoroughly flummoxed now, shrugging and collectively agreeing the gods must be trying to tell them something.

Then she saw her, the goddess Athena, invisible to the men on the battlefield below, stride over to a Trojan soldier named Laodocus. Cassandra gasped when the goddess of war did not stop her advance on the man but instead walked straight *into* him. Tears sprung to Cassandra's eyes as, with his body and mind possessed by Athena, Laodocus turned to the man next to him, an archer, and began to speak in earnest. He kept on his speech, gesturing with his hands until the archer nodded his head in agreement.

Laodocus stepped back, giving the archer room to nock his arrow.

"No," screamed Cassandra.

The men hesitated, vexed and wondering whether the warning they'd heard was inside or outside of their heads. In that moment, the archer released the arrow he'd trained on the king of Sparta. It found its target but did not strike Menelaus in the heart as intended.

Injured and in pain, he dropped to the ground, clutching the barb lodged in his war belt. The *Achaeans* immediately sprang into action, with some shielding Agamemnon as he ran to his brother's side and others quickly getting in line to form a *phalanx*.

Cassandra clamped a hand over her mouth. Had her outburst thrown the archer off his aim? Had Menelaus been meant to die this day? Relieved Menelaus was not mortally wounded, she turned on her heel and made her way downstairs. If the archer hadn't been distracted, and the arrow had pierced Menelaus's heart, the enraged Spartans would have ignored the rules of engagement. They would have not bothered to form a wall with their shields, they would have charged, storming the gates of Troy and finally sacking it right then and there.

Guilt clawed at her as she flew down the stairs and toward her room. Had it been Athena who'd protected the Greek king, or had it been Cassandra who'd betrayed her own people to save him?

CHAPTER 14

CASSANDRA SAT IN a quiet corner of the palace garden, waiting for twilight to finally succumb to darkness. The war dragged on, yet Cassandra knew there was not much time left. Doom crept ever closer, and no matter how hard she'd tried to thwart it, the world as she knew it would meet a tragic end.

Crickets chirped, oblivious to the plight of Troy. Except for Hector, no one in the royal household left the palace anymore, and the city streets remained deserted. Instead of birdsong floating on the breeze in the mornings, the terrible sounds of war filled the air.

The fighting went on all day, until the sun went down. At night, the cries of soldiers, brought inside the citadel so the healers could tend to their infected wounds, kept her awake. Not able to stand it, she would sneak down the stairs and steal away to the blessed silence of the garden, where she would sit beneath one of the olive trees and rock back and forth, praying another vision would not add insult to injury.

Cassandra stilled when she heard someone enter through the arched entryway. She peered through the quickly darkening light, watching Andromache and Hector stroll by hand in hand. She thought perhaps they'd seen her—she wasn't trying to hide her presence—but when they walked past her, continuing to discuss how thin she'd become, how dark the circles beneath her eyes had gotten, she realized they had not.

She wanted to scream at them, to let them know she was there, but she could not find the strength.

They stopped to embrace. Cassandra peered into the darkness, barely able to make out the lines of their combined silhouette.

After a long pause, Andromache said, "Don't go tomorrow."

Hector sighed, and Cassandra could hear the torment in it. Her brother was torn between honoring his wife and protecting his people. "I must."

"You've killed his closest *philoi*, Hector," continued Andromache. "Achilles will seek to avenge Patroclus."

"I would do the same."

"Please, Hector. You are all that I have."

Hot tears welled in Cassandra's eyes, and she swallowed around the lump in her throat. What about her? Didn't Andromache have her?

"You are not alone, Andromache," replied Hector. "My family loves you like their own, they always have. You are a true daughter in Hecuba and Priam's eyes."

Cassandra knew what her brother meant, and it was true. They loved Andromache in a different way than they could ever love Helen. Andromache's homeland had been sacked by the Greeks, fueling a mutual hatred. It was out of adoration for their beloved Paris that Troy accepted Helen. Her captivating beauty didn't hurt either; the people were just as enamored as their prince. They harbored no ill will toward Helen, but the only two who had grown close with her over the years was Paris, for obvious reasons, and Hector, out of pity.

"Deiphobus, Helenus... Cassandra... they consider you a sister."

"I know this," said Andromache. "And I do not mean to imply that I am ungrateful, but the love of family is different than that of true love. No man has my heart the way you do."

"Do not worry, *agapi mou*," said Hector. "The gods will protect me. All will be well."

Cassandra heard Andromache inhale deeply. There was no use arguing with Hector. He would return to the battlefield at first light.

"Speaking of your sister," said Andromache. "I worry about her mind. She regresses more with every day that passes. Sometimes it is like I have two children."

A tear slid down Cassandra's cheek, yet she did not move to wipe it away. Apollo's curse had ruined so many things, deprived her of so much. She felt foolish for thinking the reason why he'd done it was complex, for it was quite simple. If he could not have her, then no one would. They would keep their distance out of fear, labeling her a babbling lunatic, or worse—a child.

She would be rejected and abandoned, just as she had done to Apollo.

Suddenly unable to keep her eyes open, Cassandra laid down. Tired of thinking, she fell asleep to the murmuring sounds of Hector assuring Andromache everything would be all right.

Great clods of dirt flew from under the hooves of two running horses, one bay in color, the other dappled. Their coats were lathered with sweat, nostrils flared and wild. Under the pounding came the sound of turning wheels. The powerful beasts pulled a chariot, but for

*who Cassandra could not tell; the driver's gold
armor shone too bright...*

Cassandra opened her eyes, wincing at the pounding in her head. Joints protesting, she pushed herself upright, taking in her surroundings. She had fallen asleep in the garden again.

The sun was high in the sky, indicating that she had slept through the morning and into the afternoon. Her empty stomach knotted. Hecuba would no doubt call her out on her indolence.

She stood, taking a moment to comb her fingers through her tangled hair before heading into the palace to face her mother, but a wave of dizziness forced her to sit back down. A shiver ran its cold fingers along her spine as she tried not to heave, the hammering in her head growing louder, more insistent.

Cassandra waited for the vision to overtake her, but it did not come. Instead, the persistent drumming seemed to recede. She blinked, remaining still for a few moments, giving her stomach more time to settle, and to also make sure she had truly been able to avert another episode.

She had not been able to parse out the portent of this vision. It was always horses pulling a chariot, and always a warrior in golden armor, with a black plumed helmet...

And then she heard it. A war cry, closer than it'd ever been before. But it was more than that. It was a howl of rage. A keening wail of grief and despair.

"No," whispered Cassandra, shooting to her feet.

Achille's tormented scream grew louder, as did the pounding of hooves. When she realized the sound was not in her head, Cassandra ran from the garden.

"No, no, no..." she pleaded as she took the stairs to the battlements two at a time. She half expected Apollo to appear, to hinder her somehow. She lifted the hem of her dress high so the fabric would not tangle in her feet and send her crashing to the bottom with a broken neck.

The muscles in her shaking legs burned, still she ran over to the sandstone wall and, scarcely able to breathe, peered over the side. At first, she saw nothing, only heard the driving sound of hooves. But when her vision focused, she saw Trojan soldiers pouring into the courtyards of the citadel. The last of them remained outside as the gates were barred, sacrificing their lives to fend off the enemy who meant to infiltrate the city. Her gaze cut to the battlefield beyond, where the rest of the Greeks celebrated the retreat by beating their shields with weapons.

The driving rhythm of hooves grew louder, forcing Cassandra's gaze to cut to the chariot circling the citadel. It was drawn by the same horses in her dream, and she could see the dust and dirt churning beneath their hooves as they ran full bore. She saw the same glinting armor and the black plume bouncing against a backdrop of green trees and blue sky.

A strangled cry burst from her when she spied something she had not seen in her vision.

"Hector!" cried Cassandra, grasping for the wall to steady herself.

Achilles unleashed another round of rage as he exacted his revenge. Relentless, he drove the horses around the wall again and again with Hector's corpse dragging behind his chariot, cursing his name to the gods.

All strength to stand upright leaving her, Cassandra crumpled to the ground and wailed. All this time. The thrumming she'd heard had been the pounding of hooves, warning of a terrible prophecy that foretold Troy's greatest loss of all.

CHAPTER 15

CASSANDRA STARED AT the flames dancing in the braziers lighting the temple of Apollo. She refused to look at Hector's body lying in state, even though it had remained perfect and unmaimed. It was a miraculous thing, and no doubt the work of the gods, considering Achilles had dragged it around for days. He would have kept on his treacherous campaign had Priam not begged him to stop.

Distraught and desperate, her father had gone into the Myrmidon camp under the cover of darkness and pleaded for the return of his eldest son, so that he could bring him back to the palace for burial. It had taken Priam many heartfelt words and as many clever arguments for Achilles to agree. He had been so moved he'd even promised a full twelve days of armistice to perform the rites. Maybe it was because he, too, had a son, or perhaps Priam had reminded him of his own father, Peleus. Either way, Cassandra didn't care. Their beloved Hector was gone. The cold and lifeless flesh and bone under the burial shroud was no longer her brother. He lived among the gods now.

Cassandra's gaze drifted from the brazier to the crying women, and then Priam. She had never seen her father cry before, and it was a terrible sight. One she wished she did not have to experience. And then there was Paris; she could not keep her jaw from clenching when she looked at him. How dare he lament Hector's death.

It should have been him lying on that cold stone slab.

She felt as though she were a specter of Asphodel, floating aimlessly behind the procession making its way out of the temple of Apollo to Hector's final resting place, a tomb not far from the temple. She held Astyanax. Hecuba and Andromache wept, wailing and beating their chests as they walked. Cassandara's eyes remained dry. She had no more tears left, only anger. What had Achilles expected, sending Patroclus to the battlefield in his stead, wearing his armor, no less? There was no way Hector could have known it was not a fair fight, and she wondered which god had meddled to bring about this outcome.

Her only consolation was that Achilles would die soon. She'd seen it.

After the prayers had been said, and the coins for safe passage placed upon his mouth, Hector was laid to rest. The priests were the first to leave, then the seer and Polydamas, trusted advisor and friend to Hector. One by one they filed out, until only the family remained. It tore at Cassandra's heart to witness her father pulling her mother to her feet, lest she rearrange her son's grave goods several more times. Andromache, clutching a sleeping Astyanax in her arms, was led away by both Deiphobus and Helenus.

Finally, Cassandra looked at Hector. To her surprise, she was not the only one left. Paris stood across from her, staring down at their brother's lifeless mortal shell with tear swollen eyes.

It filled her with rage.

"Avenge him," hissed Cassandra, the venom in her words deadly.

Paris's gaze snapped to hers, his expression so dumbfounded it made her want to strangle him. After his divine rescue from Menelaus, Paris had not left the palace once. He'd watched from the battlements or lain in his bed, languishing between Helen's thighs, while valiant and brave Hector had fought his battle for him.

"Pierce our brother's murderer through the left heel with an arrow," she snarled, sick of the sight of him. "It's the least you can do."

Twelve days later

Paris's death had been foretold. There was nothing any of them could do, and so Cassandra did not interfere with fate by stopping him from leaving the safety of the palace and the comfort of his lover's arms to avenge Hector. Nor did she protest when he stepped outside the gates with nothing but a bow and arrow.

The entire palace had breathlessly waited for his return that first day after the armistice ended. Not Cassandra. She knew he would come strutting back, bragging of how he'd shot Diomedes with an arrow through the foot, effectively halting the fighting for the day.

She had congratulated him with the rest, pretending to be happy for his victory, as cowardly as it had been. Diomedes had called for hand-to-hand combat, but Paris had somehow convinced the hero the challenge called for weapons.

Whether he fought with fists or arrows, it did not matter to Cassandra. She would do and say anything she could to stroke his ego, so long as he kept going back to the battlefield. She had seen Achilles's downfall, and it would be with an arrow loosed by Paris. Let him believe he would be the man who would end the war, so long as he did what she'd instructed.

A few days later, by some miracle of the gods, Paris defeated Achilles. It was a relief the greatest warrior the Greeks had was gone. Much to the chagrin of everyone around her, however, Paris went back for more fighting.

It was sad to see how Helen waited each day, wringing her hands and pacing, unable to sit at the loom or take meals. Her face was pale, her frame had grown thin, and her eyes were perpetually swollen, yet she still exuded grace and beauty.

Cassandra had no doubt Helen had grown to love Paris by this point, and it did stir pity in Cassandra's heart, but not enough to go with the woman to the mountains. When Paris was carried from the battlefield back to the palace on a stretcher, writhing in pain from being struck with Philoctetes' poisoned arrow, Helen set out to find Oenone.

The nymph was the only one who could save Paris, but even though Helen begged her, she refused. Cassandra couldn't blame Oenone.

Paris should have believed her when she'd told him he would be dead to her if he left her side to go to the festival in Troy that fateful day long ago..

CHAPTER 16

CASSANDRA'S LUNGS BURNED and her chest heaved as she ran through the streets, whimpering at the pain every time her bare feet slammed onto the hard stone. She hadn't bothered to put on sandals when she'd heard the news. The Greeks were gone. The shore bore only smoking remains of their encampments, and the harbor was empty of ships.

In their place stood a massive wooden statue of a horse.

Cassandra slowed when the hard-packed earth beneath her aching feet turned to sand. She stopped to catch her breath, waiting until it evened out before continuing. Even though the waves crashed loudly, she did not want to attract the attention of the men gathered on the shore. She knew she should not be there, but she needed to see the war had finally ended with her own eyes to believe it.

The shore was littered with refuse, but it was indeed bare. Her relief quickly turned to dread when she looked up at the massive wooden horse looming above them all, the dark wood glowing like a giant ember—even in the afternoon light—from the fire burning in front of it.

Sacks of grain were scattered around the base of the statue. Cassandra drew closer, her stomach turning when she realized they weren't sacks, but men. All dead.

"What is happening?" she whispered to Helenus as she crept into place beside him.

He started, whirling toward her with a furrowed brow. "You shouldn't be here, Cassandra." He took her by the shoulders and pushed. "Go back inside."

She narrowed her eyes at him, shrugging out of his grasp. "You sound like father. I'm not going anywhere. They're gone. Now tell me what you know."

Helenus sighed, giving up his argument. He nodded at a man wearing a tattered tunic speaking with Priam, Polydamas, who held a spear in his hand, and the seer Laocoon.

"The man who speaks is Sinon, and he says after the death of Achilles, morale was low."

Cassandra could hear the pride in Helenus's voice. She lifted her chin, for she, too, was proud Hector had been avenged, even if it was by cowardly Paris. What did it matter his arrow was surely guided by a divine hand?

"And then a plague was set upon the Greeks by Apollo," said Helenus, lowering his voice. "Their general, Odysseus, called for a sacrifice and Sinon was chosen."

"He still lives?" They had all heard about clever Odysseus and his cunning strategies. It did not surprise her in the least the man would offer a comrade's life to the gods for fair winds. The Greeks were ruthless. Agamemnon had done the same, sacrificing his own daughter in exchange for something as menial as favorable sailing conditions.

"He deserted, hiding until they left."

"And *that?*" asked Cassandra. She had only to arch a brow at the wooden monstrosity for Helenus to know what she was referring to.

"A gift to Athena, for fair winds back to their lands."

It sounded all well and good, but something didn't make sense. The Greeks had fought for ten years, through the direst of conditions and countless setbacks doled out by the gods. Why would they abandon their siege now, when Troy was on the verge of collapse?

Cassandra jumped when Polydamas shouted.

"How can we be sure what you say is true?"

"Why would I start this smoking fire, alerting you to my presence, if I mean ill-will? I stand here, outnumbered, among the corpses of men who were once my friends, seeking asylum," said Sinon, going down on his knees. "Begging for mercy."

The men remained silent, but she could see the lines creasing their faces, the way their brows angled down as they looked at each other.

Cassandra wrung her hands, her breathing suddenly shallow. Were they really going to trust this man? He was Greek.

Priam inhaled a deep breath before speaking. "Suppose we do show mercy, Sinon, what do we do with this?" He gestured toward the towering effigy.

"It is not for me to say, but since you have asked, I will answer." Sinon bowed humbly. "Rather, allow me to pose a simple question. Do you think it wise to incur the wrath of Athena by dismantling her offering so soon?"

Priam's gaze shifted to the horse, considering the man's words.

"Ah, I see your conundrum," continued Sinon. "It is too big to fit inside the walls of Troy... yet it would make the perfect prize for your people, who have suffered and endured for ten long years."

"My Lord," said Laocoon, shaking his head. It seemed he had heard the same taunting lilt in the man's words, giving him the same sneaking suspicion as Cassandra. Were they the only ones who could see the man was conniving, preying upon a king's pride. "Let us discuss this matter—"

Priam lifted his hand. "Bring the horse inside. Tonight, the people of Troy will celebrate our victory."

Without warning, everything went black, and Cassandra gasped when she saw them; dirty sweating faces peering at her from the dark. Their eyes were lit by thin slits of light, illuminating the hatred in their narrowed glares.

Before Helenus could stop her, she sprinted forward, trying to form words but unable. It felt as though jagged rocks filled her throat, and only a garbled choking noise escaped. Panic seized her, stopping her in her tracks to pant like a wild animal. She looked at the men—her father—and tried again to speak.

She could manage nothing more than a panicked grunt.

One hand flew to her throat, the other pointing at the wooden horse. She must convince her father to call for his soldiers to destroy it.

They only stared at her like she had lost her mind.

Not knowing what else to do but take matters into her own hands, she lunged at Polydamas, snatching his spear. He was strong, but she had taken him by surprise, and it had come free of his grip easily.

A guttural scream tore free from Cassandra as she ran, heading straight for the terrible thing that would seal their fate. When she reached it, she gripped the shaft of the spear with both hands, so she could plunge the tip into the belly of doom. She couldn't wait to hear the screams of agony from the men inside when it pierced through one of them. Perhaps her father would believe her then.

But she was wrenched away before she could thrust the spear upward.

"No!" she cried, dropping the spear to beat on Helenus's forearms. It was to no avail, his hold on her was immovable, and when he did not release her, she began to kick, twisting around to scratch at his eyes.

He had betrayed her for the last time. If he wished to remain blind to the truth, she would be happy to oblige.

Quicker and stronger, Helenus grabbed one wrist, dropping her to grab the other.

"Burn it. Please, Helenus, they will listen to you..." pleaded Cassandra, sagging to her knees. This was his last chance to listen, and her final attempt to make him hear. *"Tell them to burn it!"*

Helenus looked down at her with pity, and she knew she had not gotten through to him.

She looked at her father, the pressure behind her eyes and in her head releasing with a torrent of tears. When he shook his head and clicked his tongue at her, she stopped resisting and let Helenus drag her away.

CHAPTER 17

THE CELEBRATIONS HAD begun right away. There was nothing for Cassandra to do but lay there and wait. Imprisoned in her room, she was forced to fall asleep to the sound of her laughing city, unaware that in just a few hours it would die.

It seemed like only minutes later when she awoke to the scraping of wood on stone. She sat upright, rubbing the sleep from her eyes so she could see her captor more clearly. She doubted they would be gentle when they killed her, but at least she would not burn.

Cassandra blinked, confused. It was not a Greek soldier, but her sister-in-law.

"Cassandra!" said Andromache, beckoning to Cassandra with one hand and holding Astyanax on her hip with the other. "Come."

Cassandra got out of bed slowly, as if she were in a dream. She could see Hecuba standing behind Andromache, holding a torch as she scanned the halls for danger. Still, she could not convince her legs to move faster. Impatient, Hecuba pushed Andromache aside and charged into the room.

"Quickly!" she said, snatching Cassandra by the arm and pulling her toward the door. "They will storm the palace soon. We need to hide."

"It will do no good," murmured Cassandra, fully awake now. "They won't stop until they find us... until we're all dead."

Hecuba let go of her arm and grabbed her shoulder.

"Shut your mouth!" she hissed, giving Cassandra a violent shake. "Do you hear me? Shut your mouth and *listen* for once."

Astyanax began to cry, and although Cassandra felt the urge to laugh at the absurdity, she stifled it, vowing instead to never say another word.

They hurried through the dim halls until they came to one of the many sitting areas in the palace. Stools dotted the center of the room and tapestries lined the walls. Hecuba pulled one of the wall hangings aside to reveal a set of stairs that led down to an underground passage. They hurried along the narrow path until they came to a door. Hecuba put her ear to it, listening for any sign of movement before pushing it open and ushering them inside.

A chill raced up Cassandra's spine when she realized they were in Hector's tomb.

Hecuba instructed Andromache to hide in one of the four alcoves before pushing Cassandra toward another. How long before the Greek soldiers defiled this tomb? And if the women did manage to remain unnoticed, how would they manage to escape with the light of day betraying them? She said naught a word as she watched Hecuba hurry over to an equally ineffective hiding spot and put out the torch.

The sounds of swords clanking and screams of pain pierced the darkness, closer one minute, farther away the next. Andromache shushed a whimpering Astyanax. Cassandra wished she could sing to him, but the risk of being heard was too great.

After a long while, Cassandra sat, hugging her knees to her chest and reminiscing of happier days, of her and Helenus running carefree through the forest to practice their archery.

Where was Helenus now? Deiphobus? Her father? Were they still alive?

Her thoughts were cut short by the shuffling of feet and panting of breath.

She bit her lip, pressing closer into the stone. She wasn't worried they would make the effort to remove the heavy stone slab and defile Hector's body, but she hoped they would take the grave goods they'd come to steal and leave, never suspecting three women and an infant were hiding in the alcoves.

Light from their torches flickered on the walls. As tempting as it was, Cassandra dared not turn her head to get a look at the assailants.

She squeezed her eyes shut when one of them grunted.

"So, this is the tomb of Troy's greatest warrior," said the man. He was young, his voice barely registering manhood. "Not so great now, is he? My father cut Hector down like a reed."

He laughed, making the arrogance in his voice even more sickening, and Cassandra clamped her mouth shut so she would not scream.

And then she stopped breathing all together, for from the darkness came a tiny voice, muffled by a hand but heard by all, nonetheless.

"Pappa?"

The world tilted on its axis as the men exploded into action, thrusting their torches into every corner of the tomb. A giant stinking beast of a man pulled Cassandra from her hiding place, as did two other dirty and blood-soaked soldiers drag Andromache and Hecuba from theirs.

Cassandra could clearly see Achille's son now. She imagined this was what the man had looked like—tall and fair-haired, lean muscled, more from fighting than food rations.

"Look what we have here," he taunted. "Women of the royal house of Troy."

"Leave us be, Neoptolomes," commanded Hecuba.

"You speak to me as though you are still a queen, Hecuba," replied Neoptolomes.

It seemed Achilles passed down his arrogant nature as well, for his son's face was contorted with a hatred Cassandra did not know a man that young could possess.

"Do what you want with the women, but the child is mine," snarled Neoptolomes.

"No," said Andromache, clutching Astyanax to her chest. "No, please!"

"Shut up, woman," said her captor.

The man tore Astyanax from Andromache's arms and handed him over to Neoptolomes.

"There, there, Hector's son," said Neoptolomes sweetly. Astyanax stopped crying at the mention of his father and looked up at the young man holding his hand with water-logged eyes. "Let's go find him, shall we?"

Andromache's captor clamped a hand over her mouth to stop her screams when Neoptolomes left the tomb with her son. He slapped her when she bit him, and when she fell to her knees, he pulled her up by her hair.

Cassandra wept, too, knowing she was powerless to stop Neoptolomes from leading Astyanax to his death. He was ensuring the son of Hector did not grow up and come looking to avenge his father.

Once Neoptolomes left, the massive brute holding Cassandra took charge.

"To the ships," he said. "Agamemnon will want first pick."

Despite her gyrations, the man holding Andromache looked skeptical, making it clear he wanted to keep her for himself.

"Ajax is right," replied the man restraining Hecuba. "Besides, that one seems a bit too feisty for you, Antilochus."

Andromache's captor nodded in agreement, and they laughed as they led the women out of the tomb. They headed toward the shore, presumably to jail them below deck until the war lords were ready to take possession of their spoils.

Hecuba remained silent, as did Cassandra, but Andromache cursed, flailing and twisting

121

so wildly Antilochus could barely keep a hold of her. When Ajax leaned over to help him control Andromache, Cassandra saw the hilt of a small dagger peeking out from the top of his war belt.

She pulled it free and plunged it into Ajax's thigh. He let go of her to pull the dagger from his leg, and when he did, she ran. His enraged bellow filled her ears as she searched for a place to hide.

Heart hammering, she dashed from overturned carts to darkened alleys, concealing herself from the tormentor who was surely looking for her. Panting, she peeked around the corner of a building. She did not see Ajax, but she did see a temple.

She bolted toward it—she would pray to Athena for help—and once inside, she raced to the statue of the war goddess and knelt.

"Just and powerful Athena," she whispered. "Save me from this torment and I shall be your humble and faithful serv—"

Dread rose the hairs on the back of her neck when there came a scuff on stone. The temple filled with an eerie silence. After several seconds, she slowly turned around.

Her heart pounded in her ears when she discovered they had not deceived her.

Rivulets of blood ran down around Ajax's knee to his shin, soaking the leather of his boot. She scooted backward, against the base of the statue as he drew closer, dropping weapons onto the stone floor with every step.

Clank.

The dagger she pierced him with.

Clank.

His sword.

Clank.

And finally, an ax.

There was nowhere left to run, nowhere to hide, and Cassandra closed her eyes, refusing to beg for mercy when he charged forward, dragging her onto her back and pinning her beneath him.

This would not be the worst of it, she knew, only the first in a long line of agonizing and demoralizing offenses committed against her until she was finally free of her pain and suffering.

CHAPTER 18

CASSANDRA WILLED AWAY hot tears as a guard pulled back the flap of a large tent. After shuffling inside, she was paraded before a group of men sitting on cushioned chairs. She tried not to gag, but the air was too heavy with the stench of musk and sour sweat. The urge to cover her mouth and nose was strong, but she resisted, not only to save herself from another beating, but because her hands were tightly bound. It would do no good.

After being inspected like livestock, the soldier shoved her toward the line of women who'd no doubt endured the same humiliation only minutes before. She tripped, whimpering in pain when she landed hard on her hands and knees. What sadistic monsters these Greeks were, prolonging the torture of women for the sheer pleasure of it.

Cassandra peered up at her mother and Andromache, but they would not look at her. She knew they desperately wanted to, but the fear of repercussion stopped them. They, too, had already suffered greatly. Their hair was coming undone, their faces bruised, dresses filthy, eyes downcast, as were the gazes of a handful of other noble women who'd been spared.

Helen, of course, was not present. She was already with Menelaus.

Cassandra climbed to her feet, panting from the effort. Every part of her was raw and stinging. She limped toward her mother, and the woman standing to one side of Hecuba moved, making space so that Cassandra could take her place as princess next to the queen.

They would live, but they were now property, to be divvied up as slaves and concubines, no matter what titles they had once held. Cassandra didn't know if she should laugh or cry.

She'd just decided she would do neither when a gruff voice broke the silence.

"Was that the last one?"

That? Was she not even seen as human to these men?

Cassandra lifted her head, her lip curled in defiance as she locked eyes with the man who'd spoken. She was as good as dead. If her life were to end here and now, so be it.

He was enormous, dressed in armor unpierced by arrow and unmarred by blade, indicating he did not take orders, but gave them. His dark beard was closely cropped over a sharp jawline and pointed chin, his brows thick and severely angled, giving credence to the sinister aura that emanated from him. He stared back at her, expressionless, until a smile crept up his pitted cheeks, revealing crooked teeth.

She knew then she should have not looked up. Not because she was scared to die, but because then she would have not piqued the interest of the king of the Greeks.

Agamemnon rose from his chair and slowly stalked forward until he was standing in front of her. She did not flinch when he reached out and gripped her chin, nor did she recoil when he pushed his thumb inside her mouth and pried it open. Cassandra glared up at him as he made an appraising noise. When he finally withdrew his hand, she snapped her teeth shut.

"Your daughter is spirited, Hecuba," he said, his eyes never leaving Cassandra. "I shall enjoy breaking her of it."

He turned and headed back toward the rest of the men. There was one among them who stood, his arms folded, his gaze fixed on Andromache. It was Neoptolomes. None of them would ever forget his face.

"I've made my choice," said Agamemnon, taking his seat once more. "Odysseus, who would you have?"

"Hecuba," said a stocky man without hesitation. He had a long, puckered scar that ran along the length of his calf. Despite his rugged appearance, he spoke gently. "My wife Penelope could use a handmaid."

Cassandra listened for a sigh of relief from her mother, but it never came. Hecuba was already plotting her escape. She was too proud to ever be another woman's servant.

"And you Neoptolomes?" Agamemnon was seated once again, fingers laced together and resting on his belly as he leaned back in his chair with one leg extended.

Neoptolomes sauntered over to Andromache. He was taller than her, but only by a few inches. With divine blood running through his veins, he would surely continue to grow to an impressive height, but that wasn't what made the scene so absurd. Andromache was old enough to be his mother, and although there were younger girls shivering among the women standing in line he could have taken, he'd chosen the wife of the man who'd killed his father.

He plucked a matted curl off her shoulder before dropping it to rest with the other tangles. "I think I'll take this one," he said. "She looks like she would bear me healthy sons."

Cassandra felt Andromache's desire to reach out and strangle the boy. It rolled off her and slammed into Cassandra with a force that stole her breath. She dared a sideways glance at Andromache, whose only response was to lift her head and stare with vacant eyes at the back of a retreating Neoptolomes.

CHAPTER 19

THE JOURNEY BACK to Mycenae was brutal. Cassandra had never traveled by boat before, and the constant rocking made her stomach queasy. Agamemnon had ordered for a sleeping mat to be put on the floor in his cabin. He'd tried to tell her it would be more comfortable than being stowed away in the bowels of the ship with the other spoils of war. But she knew better. He meant to use her whenever the mood struck, and it would be more convenient to have her close.

She did not say a word. What was there to say? She was cursed and powerless, her fate sealed long ago.

The days turned into weeks. Violent storms pummeled the ship, tossing Cassandra about the cabin. At first, she thought it might be Poseidon, angry with her vicious captor, and that she would be saved from her torment. She would gladly sink into a watery grave beneath the waves than live a life laying beneath Agamemnon.

But the ship did not capsize, and it did not surprise Cassandra that it endured. The gods had never come to her rescue before. Why would they start now?

When the sea was calm, and Agamemnon drunk, he would tell her of his sordid family history. Cassandra cringed as she listened to the stories of deceit and curses and death, but she did not offer sympathy, even when Agamemnon's voice would crack with emotion. She hated the man. Besides, she knew firsthand of curses.

Instead, she would stare at him in silence. It never failed to offend him, which gave Cassandra the tiniest sliver of satisfaction. Sometimes, when she could not stop the barest hint of a smug smile at his ire, he would strike her. Other times, it seemed to excite him and so he would climb on top of her. Either way, he always rolled over with a huff afterward and went to sleep.

After a month at sea, she was allowed to go above deck to bask in the sun. She was watched carefully, however, with Agamemnon ordering her to be tied with rope to the planks to prevent her from throwing herself overboard.

Unable to roam about as she pleased, she would close her eyes, letting the rocking of the ship lull her while she imagined being a child again, running through the trees. That would often lead to reminiscing about the day Apollo had first appeared to her, and how bright his smile had been. If she'd known then what she knew now, what would become of her, as useless as it would have been, for no one can escape the whims—or wrath—of the gods, she would have turned and ran.

Cassandra jolted awake when a boot connected with her hip and shook. She must have fallen asleep. Quickly sitting up, she blocked out the sun with a hand so she could see who stood over her.

It was Agamemnon.

"Clytemnestra will not be please I have brought you home," he said. "She's even more spirited than you." He tilted his head at her as he untied the rope around her ankle. "But I don't suppose I'll need to worry about you opening your mouth and making things worse for me."

Although the words were meant as a taunt, Cassandra could hear the nervousness in his laugh. Did this man truly care what his wife thought?

Cassandra got to her feet and hobbled over to the railing, sucking air in through her teeth at the way her raw skin stung when the wind licked at it. Her heart raced at the sight of waiting figures standing along the coastline, horns blaring in the distance. Seagulls circled overhead, doing their part in heralding the homecoming of Argos's great war hero.

Despite her trepidation, a relieved sigh escaped Cassandra's lips. If nothing else, she was looking forward to being on land again. How long that would last, she did not know.

Agamemnon was the first to disembark, and Cassandra obediently followed behind. She stood patiently as the men who'd come to greet their king rushed up to meet him, his closest friends hugging and clapping him on the back.

"Where is Clytemnestra?" said Agamemnon, scanning the crowd.

"She waits for you at the palace, My Lord." The man gestured toward a chariot. "She wants to make sure your return to the palace is as impressive as your victory over Troy."

Agamemnon nodded, smiling and lifting his chin arrogantly before climbing into the chariot. When Cassandra did not move, he commanded her to get in. Cassandra had barely stepped onto the small platform when the man handed Agamemnon the reins and he snapped them sharply. The horses bolted forward at the crack across their hind quarters, causing Cassandra to lose her footing and go crashing into the man whom she despised most in all the world.

Three enormous birds circled the battlements as they approached. At the bottom of the steps stood a woman. Her jeweled crown atop her head glittered in the sun, and Cassandra knew the woman could possess only one identity. Clytemnestra. Older sister to Helen.

Behind Clytemnestra was a rug the color of a bruise running up the steps and into the palace. The rich purplish red could only be achieved by crushing hundreds of thousands of mollusks, making the dye incredibly expensive.

Clytemnestra smiled at her husband serenely as she stepped to the side of the carpet, gesturing down at the edge of it as she bowed her head. Agamemnon puffed out his chest at his wife's suggestion his feet did not tread ordinary ground. He curved the horses to the left, so he could step onto the carpet when he exited the chariot.

A terrible screech pierced the air, drawing Cassandra's gaze upward, toward the birds circling overhead. A shiver raked its way down her spine when she realized they were not birds, but winged women, black as night.

A blade dragging across the delicate white skin of a neck flashed behind Cassandra's eyes and she knew; the Furies had ascended from the depths of Hades' realm to serve divine justice to Agamemnon.

And she had no doubt that Clytemnestra had called them.

The goddesses of vengeance growled and hissed, baring their fangs and crouching obscenely as they waited for their moment to tear Agamemnon apart for the murder of his daughter Iphigenia. One of them shrieked louder than the others, a clawed talon pointing at the unscrupulous king of the Greeks. Cassandra swallowed hard, suspecting it was Tisiphone, the Fury who avenged those killed by parricide.

Clytemnestra embraced her husband, ignoring Cassandra as she climbed down from the chariot. She would have preferred to remain unnoticed, perhaps be taken away with the horses, but the stable hand had yelled at her to get out.

"Welcome home," said Clytemnestra. "You must be weary from your travels. I have a bath waiting for you. After that, let us dine together so you may tell me of all your..." Her gaze cut over Agamemnon's shoulder to Cassandra. "Spoils of war."

Cassandra suppressed a shiver at the woman's icy glare, for in that moment, she saw Clytemnestra's plan. An image of Agamemnon slumped over as crimson water swirled around him played in Cassandra's mind.

Agamemnon cleared his throat, giving Cassandra a sideways glance. "Cassandra, princess of Troy."

Clytemnestra said nothing for several seconds, causing Cassandra's throat to go dry.

"A princess?" she finally replied. "How fitting."

Agamemnon's mood changed, growing hard in an instant. "You do not have to like it, Clytemnestra, but you will have to live with it."

Clytemnestra's gaze shifted back to her husband. "Of course."

Another rasping cry from Tisiphone made Cassandra flinch. It seemed, however, that neither Agamemnon nor Clytemnestra had heard it. If she had, she'd done well feigning ignorance to the presence of the dreadful Erinyes.

Cassandra's skin prickled with the urge to run, but there was nowhere to hide, not for her, and not for her captor. Agamemnon would pay for his crimes against his daughter and his wife, and Cassandra would never outrun the curse that would plague her until her last breath.

She could break her vow of silence and employ what little humanity still left within her and warn him of the gruesome death that would soon befall him, but she would not spare him, just as he had not spared her... or her mother and Andromache. The people of Troy.

And so, Cassandra followed behind Agamemnon as Clytemnestra led him to his doom.

CHAPTER 20

WITH A SNAP of Clytemnestra's bejeweled fingers, Cassandra was taken to a small, sparsely furnished room. There was a table with a lamp on it, but no hearth. A tiny window barely illuminated the jars stacked along the walls and on shelves, and a low stool sat tucked into one corner, presumably to reach whatever was on the very top of the shelf. Aromatic herbs—lavender, rosemary, sage—hung drying in rows.

It was a storage room, but to Cassandra, it was little more than a cell to wait out her impending doom, and so she huddled beneath the window and did just that. It might take days, perhaps only hours, but as soon as Clytemnestra had exacted her revenge on Agamemnon, she would come for Cassandra.

As much as she feared this truth, she could not deny it.

Agamemnon had been dead to Clytemnestra the moment his blade bit deep into their daughter's neck and tore away her life. She had spent the last ten years letting her hatred fester into an oozing and feverish vendetta. She had ruled Mycenae while he was away, no doubt biding her time until the day he finally returned to exact her revenge. What an insult on top of injury it must have been to be told she must accept his concubine into the home she'd kept and protected for a decade, fighting her own battles while her husband waged war across the sea.

Clytemnestra was a powerful woman. To be Agamemnon's queen, she had to be. It wasn't hard to figure out that, despite her joyful pretense at his homecoming, she would follow through with her plan to rid her kingdom of the man who valued war more than his own flesh and blood.

Mycenae was Clytemnestra's now, and there would be no chance she would let anything—or anyone—remind her of the terrible deeds Agamemnon had committed.

Cassandra startled when a woman entered the room holding a large basket and a handled jug. She gestured for Cassandra to get up, speaking in a language she didn't understand. The woman huffed as she set the basket down and pulled off the cloth covering the top. Next, she dragged the stool out from the corner and over to the table. Cassandra was so weary she considered crawling over to it when the women

138

beckoned, but she thought of how mortified her mother would be, and so she mustered the strength to get to her feet.

She sank down onto the stool, curious as to what the woman was rooting around in the basket for. She was thankful when the woman pulled out a small jar of oil and flint and not a dagger. Relieved, she sat quietly as the woman poured the oil into the lamp, lit it, and then went back to digging.

Cassandra offered the woman a weak smile when she handed her a piece of bread. She didn't know if she would get another meal, so she accepted it. She chewed slowly while the woman poured water from the jug into a bowl before wiping the dirt from her face, arms, and legs with the dampened cloth. The water was black by the time Cassandra had finished eating.

After the woman had brushed her hair and dressed her in clean clothes, she gathered her things and Cassandra was alone once more. There was nothing left to do but lay her head on the table and listen to the thunder rolling in the distance.

What was the point to all of this? To feed her and dress her in clean clothes as if she were a guest. Did Clytemnestra intend to show mercy? Did she understand that Cassandra's presence here was not of her own volition?

They were questions Cassandra could not answer, not until Clytemnestra paid her a visit.

Defeated, tears filled her eyes. They slid along her nose and dropped onto the scratched and marred wood of the table. When she could no longer bear the injustice of it all, she squeezed her lids shut and sobbed.

They flew open a moment later when a panicked cry echoed through the corridor.

Another cry, louder than the first, and it suddenly made sense why Clytemnestra had put her here; it must be close to the bath in which Agamemnon was to meet his end, and she had wanted Cassandra to hear.

Heart racing, she sat upright, listening to his furious shouts of anger turn into gurgling pleas for mercy. She swayed as her vision darkened; the bread she'd eaten threatening to make its way back up her throat.

I could run, thought Cassandra. It was true there was no door locking her in, but where would she go? Even if she did manage to escape, who would take her in? No Mycenean would dare defy their queen by hiding a Trojan. And the gods had proven untrustworthy. There would be no help from them. She was utterly alone, her kin either dead or scattered to the wind.

Instead of running, she steeled herself to see what Apollo wanted to show her.

It was not Agamemnon she saw, but Clytemnestra, lying motionless on the floor, eyes bloodshot and bulging from having been strangled by a man who stood over her.

Killed by her very own son, Orestes, for killing his father.

Cassandra trembled at the sound of Apollo's voice in her head.

An eye for an eye, blood for blood.

She covered her face with her hands.

A revenge that will go on and on... and on.

Just like the curse he had place upon her. Wasn't he also the god of plagues? His revenge was a scourge, one that would follow her wherever she went. She would speak truth, and no one would listen.

Cassandra dug her fingernails into her skin, scratching at her cheeks until she felt the sting of blood rising to the surface.

"Release me!" she moaned, her voice rasping with disuse. She clawed at her temples, grasping handfuls of hair as she lost all sense of time and space. "End my torment here and now. I beg of you, for I no longer wish to walk this earth!"

She crumpled to the floor in a heap and wept, sobbing at the loss of her agency, unable to stop what was left of who she'd once been draining away like water from the hollow shell of a woman she'd become.

Cassandra's gaze shifted to the light dancing on stone as Clytemnestra stepped into the room in a glow of torchlight.

The sound of her voice did not startle Cassandra; she was past fear. She was ready to be rid of her cursed existence. What did surprise her, however, is what the woman said.

"I believe you."

Cassandra lifted her head slowly and sighed. The thought to try and reason with Clytemnestra to spare her life was fleeting, for she had died long ago and was living no life at all.

Clytemnestra waited for it, for the begging to begin, and she tilted her head when it did not come.

"I believe you," repeated Clytemnestra, standing above her and looking down with pity.

Cassandra stared back at her in silence, knowing that the wheel of fate could not be stopped from turning.

Clytemnestra nodded, needing no words for this understanding to pass between them. She lifted her arm, the blood-soaked sleeve falling away to reveal the dagger in her hand.

The glint of metal was the last thing Cassandra saw before closing her eyes.

"Finally," whispered the princess of Troy, uttering her final word before the blade came down to end her misery.

THE END

GET A PREVIEW OF THE FALLOW AND THE FAINT

Echo giggled, peeking from her hiding spot before ducking low in the brush. She was one of the many mountain nymphs whose favorite pastime was to frolic in the forest groves and sparkling streams of Mount Cithaeron. Among them, her feet were the lightest and her laughter the most cheerful.

Like all nymphs, she was beautiful, with fair hair and eyes as clear and blue as a cloudless sky, but she was known for her storytelling best of all. Echo could capture one's attention with her comeliness and grace, to be sure, but she could hold it with her spellbinding words. It was a gift she used often, for she delighted in making others smile.

Echo squeaked when she felt a light tap on one shoulder.

"You really must find somewhere new to hide, Echo," laughed Aethra.

Echo wheeled around to see her sister standing above her with her fists planted on her hips in mock reprimand. Echo could not stop a peal of laughter from escaping when she jumped to her feet and threw her arms around her sister's shoulders.

It was like that sometimes; the joy bubbling within her could simply not be contained.

"We all know I'm better with words," replied Echo, grabbing Aethra by the hand. "Come, let's find Eudora, so the three of us can pay the goddesses a visit. You can play the lyre while I entertain them with a story."

Echo and Aethra tip-toed through the grove, careful not to crush the tiny, yellow-petaled buttercups underfoot as they searched for Eudora. They headed toward the stream gurgling in the distance, stopping to smell every patch of fragrant primrose along the way.

Echo smiled when she caught a flash of red locks through a thick grove of saplings.

"Over there," she whispered to Aethra, pointing in the direction in which she'd seen Eudora.

They carefully made their way toward the beacon of pale skin and ginger tresses in the dappled light undulating through the leaves, without making any sound at all.

As they got closer, Echo could see Eudora was standing at the base of an enormous oak, her gaze fixed upward. She pressed a finger to her lips, signaling for Aethra to remain stealthy. As they crept forward, Echo could now see that Eudora's ivory skin bore the barest hint of pink. It was obvious by the way she nervously shifted her weight from one delicate foot to the other that something high in the thick branches had caught her attention.

When Eudora's lips began to move, it was clear it was some*one* and not some*thing*.

"Who is she talking to?" whispered Aethra.

"I don't know," Echo whispered back. "A satyr, perhaps?"

Echo knew as soon as the words made their way out of her mouth it was an impossibility. Satyrs could speak, yes, but their cloven feet could not climb trees. No, it had to be a more powerful divinity to whom Eudora spoke.

Artemis visited these mountain woods from time to time.

Echo's stomach looped with the sudden fear Eudora had somehow offended the goddess of the hunt and was now trying to talk her way out of trouble. Like all goddesses, Artemis was benevolent when at peace, but break her trust or raise her ire and she could become viciously cruel in her punishment.

Echo's mind raced for what soothing words would calm the goddess enough to untangle her sister from a dangerous web, should she need to.

A gasp came from Aethra, and Echo saw to whom Eudora was speaking a moment later.

Zeus lounged high within the tree, leaning against the thick trunk with one knee up while the other hung off the enormous branch where he sat, swinging ever so slightly. His hair was long and loose, the ends lifting in the crisp mountain breeze. Smooth, high cheekbones gave way to a beard surrounding full lips that held a languid smile.

What was the king of the gods doing in the woods? Convalescing in a tree, at that.

Echo swallowed hard when his piercing gaze, as blue as the deepest mountaintop spring, turned toward her and Aethra, who both stood stunned.

Echo reached out, pulling Aethra down into a curtsey and then bowing deeply herself. When they rose, he was grinning broadly at them.

"Beautiful day is it not, my ladies?" he said, gesturing toward the sky before cupping his knee casually. The bottom of his tunic had settled into the crease of his hip, revealing a muscular upper thigh.

Echo blinked. This was no time to be lost in stupor.

"A lovely day, indeed," she said, smiling brightly. "What brings you down from mighty Olympus to our humble little mountain, Your Majesty?"

Eudora shot Echo a side-long look. Her sister's lips were pushed out into the slightest pout, indicating she was irritated by the interruption.

"Why, what else?" He inhaled, as if to prove it was truly the bracing mountain air he sought. "I came down for a bit of time to myself, and just so happened upon your lovely sister."

Echo continued to smile politely, even though she knew the truth. Zeus's quest had nothing to do with admiring the beauty of field and stream, and everything to do with ogling the nymphs who dwelled among them.

But she dared not call out the king of the gods for his true intentions.

"It's no wonder," said Echo, switching her gaze to Eudora, "She is the loveliest of us all." She stepped toward her sister, intent on pulling her away. "But it's time for us to entertain the goddesses, and so she must be going."

Echo's fingertips brushed the soft bare skin of Eudora's arm just as she stepped out of reach.

"I do not wish to be rude to His Majesty," said Eudora, glancing up at Zeus. "Do go on without me. I'm sure the goddesses will not even notice my absence."

A ghost of a smile tipped Zeus's lips. "Yes, do go on without Eudora," he said. "I shall make sure no harm befalls her, for I quite like her company."

Echo looked back at Aethra with arched brows, but she got no answer to her silent question, and so she tried a final time. The goddesses, especially Zeus's wife, Hera, noticed everything.

Echo cleared her throat, aiming to work her magic, but before she could get the words out, Zeus spoke.

"Go now," said Zeus. His tone was not harsh, but there was no mistaking it was the end of the discussion. Eudora would not be going anywhere. "And be sure to entertain them with a very, *very* long story, Echo."

The Author

Forever a fan of fairytales, folklore, and mythology, Kerri brings life to the mythological characters you know and love... or love to hate.

Kerri lives in Michigan with her husband, son and cat they lovingly but aptly refer to as The Maleficence. Mel for short. If Kerri isn't raking leaves or shoveling snow, she's either reading, writing or has fled her evil to-do list and fallen down an Internet rabbit hole... Or possibly just fallen and can't get up.

For news and updates about upcoming releases, sign up for Kerri's newsletter at kerrikeberly.com. For an inside look at the day in the life of a crafty crochet-addicted, DIY-loving, Greek mythology-obsessed author, follow her on Facebook, Instagram, and TikTok.

.

Milton Keynes UK
Ingram Content Group UK Ltd.
UKHW011042150724
445326UK00015B/14